TEMPTING DEVIL

USA TODAY BESTSELLING AUTHOR

T.K. LEIGH

TEMPTING DEVIL

Published by Carpe Per Diem Publishing, Inc

Cover Design: Cat Head Media, Inc.

Cover assets:

Used under license from Deposit Photos and Adobe Stock © 2024

Copyright © 2024

All rights reserved.

BOOKS BY T.K. LEIGH

ROMANTIC SUSPENSE
The Saint Trilogy
Cruel Saint

Tempting Devil

Final Vendetta

The Temptation Series
Temptation

Persuasion

Provocation

Obsession

The Broken Crown Trilogy
Royal Creed

Fallen Knight

Broken Crown

For a free eBook, sign up for T.K.'s newsletter.

Some of T.K. Leigh's books may contain content that could be triggering for sensitive readers. For a full list of content warnings for each book and/or series, please visit her website by scanning the code below.

CHAPTER ONE

Samuel

Five Years Ago

The reflection of the warm, golden light danced and shimmered on the sleek surface of the diamond, making it sparkle against the dimly lit backdrop of my home office.

There were a thousand things I should have been doing besides staring at this engagement ring. That was the thing no one ever told me about success — with success came the responsibility to ensure the livelihoods of each and every one of my employees.

But right now, all I could think about was Imogene.

And how it felt like my plans for giving her this ring were slipping away.

I thought it would go off without a hitch. I'd surprise her with a belated birthday trip to Hilton Head now that she was done with finals. We'd take Ollie, since she loved that dog as much as I did. I'd attach the ring to his collar, then have him run up to her. When she'd notice the ring box on his collar, I'd drop down to one knee and ask her to be my wife.

But it didn't look like that would be happening this weekend.

Unbeknownst to me, my best friend and business partner — who also happened to be one of Imogene's closest friends — *also* planned a surprise for her. An elaborate party at The Swan House in Atlanta he bought out for the occasion, costing him thousands of dollars.

Imogene didn't even like parties, especially the type of party Liam liked to throw, inviting anyone who was someone to be there.

I hoped to use this as a way to convince her to finally tell him the truth about us, like I'd been begging her to do since her actual birthday.

While I wanted to keep what we had a secret from my best friend in the beginning, too, I now regretted ever making that agreement. Wished I'd thrown caution to the wind and refused to hide what we had from everyone.

I thought I was doing the right thing. I saw the way Liam looked at her. Knew his feelings for her went beyond that of a close friend. A part of me hoped he'd eventually get over it once he realized she didn't return those feelings.

That never happened.

Now, I was tired of having to hide what I shared with Imogene because she was scared of how Liam might react. Of losing him as a friend. Would she *ever* want to tell him the truth?

Or was she content for me to remain her dirty little secret?

I thought proposing would show her how serious I was.

Now, after our argument earlier today, I questioned everything.

Even if I convinced her to take this next step, was this what our marriage would be like? Her always choosing Liam over me because of some misplaced responsibility she felt toward him, all because her sorry excuse for a sperm donor took Liam's mother from him?

From the beginning, I thought their friendship was toxic. After witnessing how much he manipulated her over the past year, that feeling had only grown stronger.

What would it take for her to see what everyone else did?

The shrill chirping of my cell broke the silence, and I shut the velvet box, tucking the ring back into the top drawer of my desk.

Grabbing my phone off the surface, I clicked on the incoming text from Jonah, one of the teenagers I mentored at the local community center I founded a few years ago when my gaming platform took off.

If it weren't for this kind of program, I wouldn't be where I was today. There was no question in my mind about starting a program like this as my own way of doing something useful with the money I'd made, instead of simply watching it grow in my bank account.

JONAH:

The asshole came home drunk again.

I cursed under my breath, clenching my jaw.

Like most kids in my program, Jonah had a rough home life — an abusive father who drank a lot, then took it out on everyone else. This was the reason he wanted to learn martial arts. Not to be able to hurt his asshole father, but to learn how to take a punch so his mother didn't have to.

As I learned early in life, calling the police didn't always help in these types of situations. Especially for kids who lived in neighborhoods where violence and crime ran rampant. Even if the cops did make an arrest, it rarely helped. The instant they returned home, things would be much worse than they were before. Instead, you just learned to take the abuse as you counted down the days until you could finally be free.

ME:

Are you okay? How about your mom?

JONAH:

I was able to distract him long enough for her to get out with the younger ones.

I squeezed my eyes shut. I hated that this was the world Jonah was forced to grow up in. I didn't have it much better, but at least I had my foster brothers to depend on when shit got bad.

I was the only person Jonah had.

ME:

Want me to call someone?

I didn't know why I bothered asking. His answer was always the same. Just like mine was. Which was why I hadn't intervened.

Yet.

Instead, I'd done everything I could to teach Jonah how to defend himself and the rest of his family.

JONAH:

Can you come get me?

I checked the time to see it was almost midnight. It would probably take me about twenty-five minutes to get to his neighborhood. I needed to wake up early for an important meeting with the heads of a company that had been trying to buy the firm from Liam and me, which I resisted at every turn. Still did.

But if Jonah needed me, I'd be there for him.

Like I wished someone had been there for me all those years I hid in my room praying I wouldn't hear the floorboards creak near my door.

ME:

Will you be okay until I can get there?

JONAH:

I'm out of the house, but I'd rather not sleep on the street tonight, even if it's safer.

I cursed again, hating he thought it was safer to sleep on the street in a rough section of Atlanta than in his own bed.

ME:

Drop a pin and I'll be there as soon as I can.

Without wasting another second, I jumped to my feet and grabbed my keys. As I made my way toward the front door, I paused by the hallway closet and opened the safe, retrieving my pistol. Then I dashed out of my house and into my SUV.

The streets of my residential neighborhood were relatively quiet this late at night. Growing up in foster care, I never could have imagined owning such a nice house in the upscale Buckhead area of Atlanta. While some people in the foster care system had great placements, I wasn't so lucky. Instead, each placement only seemed to get worse. The only thing that saved me was martial arts and wrestling. Because of that, I was awarded a full scholarship to college. If that had never happened, I wasn't sure where I would have been today.

Probably in prison.

Or worse.

As I drove through the city, cozy residential neighborhoods eventually gave way to dilapidated buildings with boarded-up windows and graffiti-covered walls. I hated that this was all Jonah had ever known. I could only hope my program did for him what a similar one did for me.

Despite his circumstances, Jonah was a bright kid. Demonstrated a keen mind, especially when it came to computers, which was why Henry, one of my foster brothers and a computer genius, took him under his wing, as well. Hopefully, between the two of us in his corner, he would break the cycle.

After navigating a few more blocks of rundown buildings, I pulled into the parking lot where Jonah dropped the pin, verifying I was in the right place. I had no idea why he was here. In the past, whenever he ran into trouble, he'd hide out in a church. But tonight, he was somewhere in an old shopping plaza, the buildings looking like they'd been vacated long ago.

I parked in the empty lot near the building and scanned the area for Jonah, not immediately seeing any sign of life.

Fishing my cell out of my pocket, I fired off a quick text.

ME:

Here.

Within a few moments, a hooded figure emerged from the side of the building and made his way toward me, a gun clutched in his hand. I didn't even want to ask how Jonah came to own a gun, considering he was under eighteen and couldn't buy one legally in the state yet. Considering where he lived and his current situation, I couldn't blame him for wanting one to be on the safe side.

As he grew close, I unlocked the car, continually scanning my surroundings. A chill trickled down my spine, something unsettling filling me with an odd sense of premonition. The sooner I got Jonah out of here, the better.

With quick motions, he opened the passenger door and slid into the car, not removing his hoodie.

Nor did he lower his gun.

In fact, he raised it, pointing it at me, its black metal glinting in the moonlight.

My pulse raced as I tried to comprehend what was happening. "Jonah, what are—"

I stopped short when he finally looked up.

Only it wasn't Jonah.

The piercing gaze that met mine belonged to my best friend.

"What are you doing, Liam? Where's Jonah?" Panic raced through me as I stole a glance toward the glove box where I'd stashed my gun.

A sly smirk crept across Liam's mouth, revealing a side of my friend I'd never seen before. "Don't worry. He'll be well taken care of."

Before I had a chance to react, a loud bang reverberated in the car as a searing pain tore through my body. I slumped against the seat, my world going dark.

CHAPTER TWO

Imogene

Present Day

My chest constricted, a weight suffocating me, freezing me in place. Nothing made sense. Not after hearing that name... *Samuel Tate.*

It echoed in my head, a never-ending nightmare I couldn't wake up from, no matter how hard I'd tried.

I thought moving to California would give me the fresh start I desperately needed, an escape from the overwhelming grief of Samuel's death.

But now, after five years, a glass with his fingerprints was found at Alton's cabin?

How was I supposed to process that information? What could it mean?

A part of me always held on to a tiny glimmer of hope he might still be alive. Without a body, that was all it was.

Over the past few weeks, however, I let go of the idea. Let go of *him*. Moved on from the constant pain of losing Samuel.

Now this revelation had shattered everything. Could it be possible? Could Samuel still be alive?

The notion sent chills down my spine, obliterating the fragile peace I'd finally found after years of turmoil.

I didn't know how, but I somehow managed to force my heavy legs to carry me down the hallway of Liam's house. Each step required a herculean feat, my world spinning around me, threatening to throw me off.

As I emerged into the foyer, Liam's housekeeper approached, scanning my appearance in concern.

I had no idea what I looked like right now, but I must have looked rattled. Like I'd just seen a ghost.

In a way, I had.

"Is everything okay, Ms. Prescott?" she asked in an accented voice, her tone soft and soothing.

But nothing could soothe the confusion swirling within me.

"Sure. Yeah. He's busy. I'll reach out to him later," I rushed out, practically running toward the front door.

I could feel her suspicion watching me as I left the house.

Samuel often teased me for having a horrible poker face. Said I wore my emotions on my sleeve for all to see. After overhearing what I just did, I was pretty sure even a complete stranger, like Liam's housekeeper, could sense I was teetering on the edge of having a breakdown.

I jumped into my car and peeled out of the elaborate driveway, speeding all the way back to La Jolla. I wasn't even sure *how* I got home, the thirty-minute drive going by in a blur as I contemplated every single scenario why Samuel's fingerprints could have been found on that glass.

And why Liam sounded petrified over the notion.

When I walked into my townhouse, Ollie bounded toward me with his usual excitement, his tail wagging and mouth hanging open. Normally, I looked forward to seeing my sweet boy after being away from him all day. Today, the sight of him was yet another reminder of Samuel.

"Want to go out?" I asked Ollie rather unenthusiastically.

He must have picked up on my mood, tilting his head to the side and studying me. If he could talk, he'd probably ask if I was okay.

The truth was, I wasn't sure *what* I was. Other than fucking confused.

"Come on, pal." I moved through the living room and headed toward the back door.

The wooden panels creaked under my feet as I swung the door open, allowing the ocean breeze to rush in.

Ollie bolted onto the deck, and I followed him down the steps to the fenced-in back yard. It wasn't as much space as he was used to back in Atlanta, but considering where I lived, it was better than not having any yard at all.

As I threw Ollie's ball for him, I continued to replay the conversation I overheard, my thoughts tangled and twisted. I cleared my mind, trying to keep emotion out of it and think about everything rationally. Only focus on the facts.

And the only facts I *did* know were that investigators found a glass on the coffee table at Alton's cabin containing Samuel Tate's fingerprints. That it wasn't the only glass there, either, which was why investigators found it odd, considering Alton was supposedly alone when he took his life. That Liam and James both sounded nervous about the idea of someone purposefully leaving a glass with Samuel's fingerprints for investigators to find.

But why? What would that have to do with them?

I had no idea, but I needed to find out.

And I knew where to start.

"Come on, Ollie. Want some dinner?"

He darted past me and up the deck, eagerly wagging his tail as he sat obediently at the back door.

When I opened it for him, he dashed inside, dancing circles in front of me, causing me to trip over him several times during the short walk toward the kitchen. After pouring his kibble into his bowl, I filled a glass with red wine and took a sip.

I had a feeling I'd need the wine to get through what I was about to do.

As Ollie ate, I slipped down the hallway and into my office, heading toward the stacks of Banker's boxes piled high in one corner, looking for one in particular. After finding it, I carried it into the living room and set it on the coffee table.

With my wine glass clutched tightly in my hand like a security blanket, I simply stared at the box for what felt like an eternity.

It had been years since I last looked at the contents of this particular box. I almost didn't bring it with me when I moved, hoping to finally leave my past behind me. But something prompted me to pack it at the last minute, as if a part of me knew it wasn't over. That there were still too many unanswered questions.

After taking a fortifying sip of wine, I sat on the floor in front of the box and lifted the lid, immediately assaulted with a wave of memories of what once was.

Memories of a past I thought I'd moved on from.

Memories that now threatened to break me all over again.

CHAPTER THREE

Gideon

"Any changes?" I asked as I slipped into what had become Henry's makeshift command center in my house. The room was filled with screens connected to computers via a mess of cables, a faint hum filling the air from the array of equipment.

I couldn't remember the last time he'd gone into his actual office. Then again, when he agreed to help, he told me he didn't want any of his actions to hurt his company or employees. He'd taken a temporary leave of absence, using his own time and resources to help me.

"They're still pissing themselves, more or less," Henry answered, his fingers flying across the keyboard. "But they haven't made any significant moves yet."

"Good." I collapsed onto the leather sofa and chugged a bottle of water, sweat clinging to my skin.

I'd just spent the past few hours going to town on a punching bag in my home gym. Not just to stay in top physical condition, but to mentally prepare myself for the next phase of my plan.

Alton may have been dead, but I wasn't done yet.

If anything, I was just getting started.

Alton was an easy target.

James and Liam wouldn't be.

Especially James, considering he was a United States Senator. While he didn't have the same level of protection afforded to the president, he still had more security than the average citizen.

But that wouldn't stop me.

He was the reason Jonah was arrested and falsely accused of my murder. He used his influence as a prosecutor to ensure that Jonah would never have his day in court.

For that, I'd make sure James suffered much worse than Alton Sinclair. In the grand scheme of things, Alton's death was quick and painless. While his death was driven partly out of revenge, there was a greater purpose behind it.

To send a message.

By the way James and Liam were pacing around

Liam's opulent office, they'd received that message loud and clear.

"They're worried that, with the fingerprints being found at the scene of Alton's suicide, the police may reopen the investigation into Samuel's death," Henry explained. "Considering James is no longer a DA, he may not be able to influence the investigation like he did last time."

I wiped a towel along my face, unable to stop the grin from spreading on my mouth as I watched the two men panic over what police might find if someone actually did a thorough investigation into what happened to me. It was even better than the look of dread on Liam's face when he learned Alton's recent trading advice was shit, causing him to lose millions.

"There's one thing you should know," Henry stated after a moment, his voice guarded.

I sat up straighter. "What's that?"

He hesitated, his tongue darting out to moisten his lips. "Imogene showed up about a half-hour ago."

I nodded, not all that surprised by this.

While she hadn't spoken to Liam since their argument last weekend, she wasn't heartless. In fact, she probably cared too much for her own good. Which was why it didn't shock me to learn she would have gone to see Liam upon learning about Alton's death, despite their differences.

As much as I hated the idea of her spending any time with Liam, considering what I knew about him, I couldn't outright forbid it. Not without revealing everything.

And I had no plans to do that.

Instead, I ensured Imogene's safety by keeping a close eye on her at all times.

"She was only there for a few minutes, though," Henry added. "And she never spoke to Liam."

This caught my attention. "She didn't? Did he turn her away?"

This seemed extremely out of character. Liam always made time for Imogene, regardless of what he was doing. Not because he cared about her, but because it was another opportunity to sink his claws even deeper into her.

"No." He hit a few keys on his keyboard, and the monitor in front of me switched to display six different camera feeds from Liam's security system that Henry had hacked into.

While he already had cameras in many of the public areas of the house, there weren't any in his office, an issue we remedied when his security system was supposedly malfunctioning during the golf tournament last weekend.

After a few seconds, Imogene's SUV pulled in front of the entrance and the housekeeper welcomed her. I watched her move from one camera to the next as she made her way down the hallway and toward the office.

But she didn't knock. Instead, she hesitated outside, leaning closer to the door. After several drawn-out seconds, her body stiffened and she backed away, her spine hitting the wall behind her. She placed her hand over her chest as she drew in deep breath after deep breath, her wide eyes making it seem like whatever she just heard was suffocating her.

Then she spun on her heels, practically bolting out of the house.

"What did she hear?" I asked timidly, although I was already fairly certain what it was.

"This."

My stomach twisted into knots as he clicked the spacebar and a new feed appeared, this one displaying Imogene walking down the hallway on one side and James and Liam talking in his office on the other.

"Maybe it's an old glass," Liam said, tugging at his tie. By the sheen on his normally polished face, he looked like he'd been sweating. "One that hasn't been washed lately."

"One that was conveniently left on the coffee table next to Alton's?" James retorted, his voice heavy with disbelief as he stood by the window, looking out over Liam's property.

"What other possible explanation is there?" Liam

threw his hands up as he paced the length of the room. Stopping in front of his desk, he grabbed his rocks glass and guzzled the liquid before slamming it back down. "Somebody must have made a mistake. Have them run the prints again."

"They already have," James snipped back, moving toward Liam. "Twice. Along with a few other items found in close proximity to Alton's body. Initially, it was to confirm the cause of death, but the second glass on the coffee table stumped them, so they ran it to see if someone else was in the room with Alton." He lowered his voice. "To see if maybe *you* were in the room with him, considering...recent events."

"I told you!" Liam roared, his voice echoing off the walls. "I have no idea how that damn body ended up on my boat. I haven't been to that marina in months. There's no record of me using my access card at the gate."

I couldn't help but chuckle at the irony of it all. These two men conspired to kill me and let someone else take the blame for it. Now they were experiencing the same fate. At least Liam was.

"I believe you," James replied calmly. Or as calm as he could in this situation. "But that doesn't change the evidence they uncovered in Alton's cabin."

Silence hung heavy between them, broken only by the ominous ticking of the grandfather clock standing watch in the corner of the room.

"What does this mean?" Liam asked finally, collapsing onto the couch. He ran a trembling hand over his weary face, resigned to the reality that his carefully built house of cards was starting to crumble around him.

"Either someone planted his fingerprints there to fuck with us," James began.

"Or..." Liam prodded, lifting his eyes.

"Or Samuel Tate's back from the dead."

I looked from the feed of the office to the one of the hallway, watching Imogene back up until she hit the wall behind her.

I knew there was a strong possibility James would use his influence to uncover every detail about Alton's death, despite the police not releasing any of this information to the public yet.

Nothing could have prepared me for the pure agony consuming Imogene when she learned that my — *Samuel's* — fingerprints were found on a glass at Alton's cabin.

"Now what?" Henry asked, cutting through the silence.

"What do you mean?"

"What's your plan now?"

I stared at the paused screen for several beats. At Imogene's pained expression. But I quickly brushed it off, pretending it didn't gut me.

"Same as before," I replied, forcing confidence into

my voice through the doubt and guilt gnawing at my insides.

"And if she figures out who you really are?" Henry arched a brow.

"Look at me." I gestured at my face. "Do I even remotely resemble Samuel Tate?"

"No, but—"

"But nothing. I knew there was a chance Imogene would learn about this when I made the decision to plant my DNA at Alton's cabin. It was a risk I was willing to take in order to make these assholes pay."

"And Imogene?"

"What about Imogene?" I asked guardedly.

He crossed his arms in front of his chest, the sleeves of his t-shirt stretching from the motion. "How are you going to deal with her knowing the truth?"

"She doesn't know the truth."

He opened his mouth to argue, but I quickly cut him off.

"All she knows is a glass containing Samuel's DNA was found at Alton's cabin."

"And if she somehow learns you *are* alive?"

I gritted my teeth, pushing down my growing unease. "She won't."

Henry narrowed his gaze at me. "Imogene is smart. You may have a different face, but she knows your heart, Sam."

I opened my mouth to chastise him for disregarding the one rule I made him swear to when we started down this path. But he cut me off before I could.

"She knows what's inside you. Knows your soul. What makes you tick. Your face may have changed, but your soul is still somewhere in there. And I've been seeing more and more of the old you since you started spending time with her. Since you started allowing yourself to be human again. I have a feeling the more time you spend with her, the more pieces of the old you will return until you'll no longer be able to deny who you are. That you *are* Samuel." He paused, searching my expression for any sign of recognition or acknowledgment of this truth.

But I remained stoic, my walls firmly in place.

"Samuel Tate is dead." I stood, pinning him with a glare. "And he will remain dead long after this is over. Nothing will change that." I turned toward the door.

"Regardless of whether Samuel Tate *is* dead or alive," Henry began, forcing me to pause in my tracks and face him, "she may find out the truth eventually. If you want a future with her, don't you think it would be best—"

"*There is no future with us!*" I roared as I advanced on him, barely an inch separating us.

I wasn't sure if my sudden surge of anger was because Henry's incessant line of questioning had finally become too much, or because of the harsh reality that there could never be a future between Imogene and me. Not now that I'd started down this path.

"Why do you say that?" Henry pressed, undeterred by my outburst, like always.

"I'm here for one reason and one reason only," I reminded him in a firm tone. "Revenge. Nothing more."

"So you don't care about Imogene?" Henry scoffed, the disbelief heavy in his voice.

"I can't."

"But you do, despite what you may wish. Just like she's never stopped loving you, you've never stopped loving her."

"Stop," I growled, but Henry didn't listen, refusing to back down.

"You could have a future together."

"A future?" I scoffed.

"It's not too late."

"I'm a killer, Henry. There *is* no future for us. Not with who I am." I met his gaze. "She's better off without me."

He tilted his head, studying my expression with the same analytical stare I'd come to expect from him. "Do you really believe that?"

"I *know* that."

He glowered at me for several long moments, his jaw

ticking, waiting for me to change course. But I wouldn't. Not over this.

"Then stop seeing her."

"What?" I blinked repeatedly, his words catching me off guard.

"I've held my tongue about you using Imogene. But I won't do it anymore. Not when I've just witnessed for myself the emotional toll this is taking on her. You said no one innocent would get hurt."

He gestured toward the screen still paused on Imogene's anguished expression as she clutched her chest.

"Well, she's innocent, Sam. Yet, she's still hurt. And it's only going to get worse the more time you spend with her. The more *lies* you tell her."

I swallowed down the guilt festering inside me as I stared into her eyes, wishing I could wrap her in my arms and assure her it would all be okay. But I couldn't. Not when I was the cause of her current heartache.

Drawing in a deep breath, Henry returned his gaze to mine. "You know I love you like a brother and I understand why you're doing all of this. But maybe you need to stop being so worried about protecting her from Liam. Instead, maybe the person you should be protecting her from is you."

CHAPTER FOUR

Imogene

"What the hell is going on here?"

I snapped my head up, momentarily disoriented as I took in my surroundings with bleary eyes.

The sun had begun to set, casting a dim orange glow over the living room. How long had I been going through this box of memories? Long enough for Melanie to not only show up at my townhouse, but also let herself in.

Since getting home, I'd been consumed with going through every article and report I'd saved about Samuel's death. Then I got the great idea to see if there had been any recent articles. As expected, there weren't any, apart from the obligatory public relations stories about the annual golf tournament Liam hosted in honor of his murdered friend — the most recent one being last weekend.

Somewhere along the way, I switched gears and began researching how long fingerprints could last on objects, specifically glass. Unfortunately, I didn't find anything definitive. The general consensus was that it all depended on the environment and what elements it had been exposed to. Considering the glass was found in a temperature-controlled environment with low humidity and wasn't exposed to any outdoor elements, it was entirely possible the prints could have been from before Samuel died.

But why was it left on the coffee table beside the glass Alton had been drinking out of? Wasn't that suspicious?

Or was I just grasping at straws again? Holding on to the tiniest sliver of hope that Samuel was still alive when all rationale told me he was gone?

"Is there a reason you're going through all of this?"

"Mel, I... What are you doing here?" I pulled myself to my feet, stretching my neck from side to side, my muscles sore from spending the past few hours hunched over. "Weren't you going to check on Liam?" I asked, trying to divert her attention away from the papers scattered on the coffee table and floor.

"I did. Like I thought *you* were, too."

"Shit." I ran a hand over my face. "I meant to call, but I got...distracted."

"Apparently," she snipped back with an exaggerated roll of her eyes as she walked into the kitchen to pour herself a glass of wine.

Once she took a sip, she leaned against the island, crossing a single arm in front of her stomach. It was obvious she came straight from work. Her tall and slender frame was dressed in a crisp, white button-down shirt tucked into a pencil skirt, her dark hair falling in waves down to her mid-back. A pair of animal print heels completed the look. It was a stark contrast to my current appearance of yoga pants and a t-shirt, my blonde hair piled on top of my head in a messy bun.

"Want to tell me why you're surrounded by articles about Samuel?" Her expression softened as she moved toward me. "I thought you were past this."

I parted my lips, searching my brain for a way to explain this without sounding like I was losing my mind.

"Not that you need to forget him entirely," she added quickly. "I'm not saying that. But you can't keep doing this to yourself, Ginny. I get that this time of year is hard, since it's around the fifth anniversary of his death. I thought you were only going to look forward. Not backward. Thought you were going to stop clinging to a ghost."

"I know." I released a long breath. "I just..." I licked

my lips, then scrunched my brows. "Did Liam say anything when you saw him?"

She gave me a quizzical look. "Liam?"

"Did he mention anything about Alton's cabin?"

"What specifically? Because when I was over there, Liam wasn't exactly in a talkative mood."

I lowered myself onto the couch, moving stacks of papers out of the way so she could join me. Once she did, I faced her.

"I went over his place right after I got off the phone with you."

"His housekeeper told me, but said you weren't there for more than five minutes and that you seemed upset when you left. She thought it was because of Alton." She snorted a laugh. "I had my doubts about that. Not that you're a heartless bitch, but you were never too close to Alton. And since it appears you've spent the past few hours taking a trip down memory lane..." She waved at the papers in front of me, "I have a feeling it's something else." She leaned closer, her expression awash with sincerity. "What's going on, Gin?"

"I overheard Liam and James talking," I admitted with a sigh. "They sounded...anxious. At least Liam did. Apparently, the police discovered two glasses on Alton's coffee table they found suspicious, considering Alton had allegedly been alone all day."

"Do they think he was murdered?"

"I don't know."

"Then—"

"The second glass had Samuel's fingerprints on it," I blurted out.

She straightened, blinking several slow blinks as she processed this information. Based on her silence, she was just as stunned to learn about this as me.

"And you...what?" She narrowed her gaze. "Think he's still alive?"

"I don't know what to think," I answered honestly. "One minute, I look at all the overwhelming evidence that says Samuel died, as well as the fact that it's not completely impossible to find fingerprints on a glass after five years under the right conditions. Trust me. I've learned more about fingerprints in the past few hours than I ever thought possible."

"And the next?" she prodded.

I pinched my lips together, fighting against the emotions threatening to overwhelm me once more. "The next, I still hold on to a tiny sliver of hope that he might still be alive," I squeaked out.

She nodded, peering into the distance as she sipped her wine. "Did you ask Liam and James about it?" She turned her gaze back to mine.

"I never spoke to them. After overhearing them mention Samuel's fingerprints being found at Alton's cabin, I sort of freaked. So I left and came here." I chewed on my bottom lip, stealing a glance her way before finally mustering the courage to ask, "Do you think it's suspicious?"

She gave me a quizzical look. "What?"

"The glass. What are the chances that Alton would kill himself and, when the police investigate, they find Samuel's fingerprints on a glass?"

She pushed out a long sigh and placed her hand over mine. "You know I love you. And you know how much I adored Samuel. But like you *just* said, there are mountains upon mountains of evidence supporting his death. Hell, I'm looking at mountains upon mountains of evidence supporting his death." She gestured at the newspaper clippings, investigative reports, and photographs littering my living room.

"Is finding *that* particular glass suspicious? Maybe. Or perhaps it's just a coincidence. In the extremely rare and improbable event Samuel *did* survive and *is* still alive, where has he been all these years? Not to mention, he loved you, Imogene. No way would he just disappear from your life without an explanation. As much as it sucks, Samuel was shot and killed. Any fingerprints found on a glass have to be from before he died. It makes more sense than the alternative that Samuel's been alive all this time and hasn't contacted you. Don't you think?"

I pushed out a defeated breath, briefly closing my

eyes as I allowed my best friend to wrap an arm around me.

"You're right," I admitted, unable to deny all the valid points she made. Things I hadn't really considered until she brought them up.

"I usually am," she said with a wink before squeezing me tighter.

It was moments like these I was grateful to have someone like Melanie to talk some sense into me. Bring me back down to reality. Remind me what was possible and what wasn't.

And Samuel still being alive and never reaching out?

That was impossible.

At least that was what I needed to keep telling myself.

CHAPTER FIVE

Imogene

"Are you sure you'll be okay?" Melanie asked as I walked her out to my front porch later that evening.

"I'm fine. Promise." I squeezed her bicep. "Like you said. Samuel had been to Alton's cabin on numerous occasions before he died. His fingerprints must be left from one of his visits."

"It's not that I don't wish they *could* be recent. I'd give anything for him to still be alive. But you can't keep putting yourself through this. You came out here to get a fresh start and put the past behind you. You've finally met someone who I think has helped."

As if on cue, a sleek Jaguar convertible rolled to a stop in front of my townhouse, and I couldn't fight the smile that tugged on my lips as Gideon Saint stepped out. His tall and muscular body was dressed in a perfectly tailored black suit, his dark hair styled in a sexy, disheveled way.

It was a stark contrast from last night when he showed up at my door at three in the morning wearing jeans and a hoodie. Now, he was back to being Gideon Saint, the mysterious billionaire who saved me in a dark alley a few weeks ago.

"Please don't throw it away over a ghost," Melanie whispered, then turned, heading down the front steps of my porch.

"You don't have to leave," I said, following her. "You can stay over if you want."

"I appreciate the offer, but there's a special place in hell for people who stand in the way of their best friend getting some good dick, especially when you need it. And after today, I have a feeling some good dick is *much* needed."

I barked out a laugh, grateful for Melanie's unique ability to always lighten a tense situation.

"Plus, I have an early meeting tomorrow. Traffic will be much better tonight than in the morning. Gotta love Southern California."

"Drive safe," I said as I hugged her.

"Always." She squeezed back, releasing me when

Gideon approached, his expression awash with sincerity as he swept me into his arms.

A few hours ago, it felt like my world had been tilted on its axis. I didn't think anything or anyone would ever make me feel better. But being in Gideon's embrace did precisely that. It set everything right again. As if this was where I was meant to be — wrapped in his strong arms, surrounded by his comforting scent and warmth.

Not chasing after a ghost.

"How are you?" he asked, clutching my cheeks and forcing my gaze to his.

"Okay," I said with a soft smile.

He surveyed my demeanor, his blue eyes searching for any sign I was lying.

But I wasn't. I *was* okay.

"Good," he replied, sounding almost relieved as he touched a soft kiss to my lips, lingering only a moment or two before shifting his attention toward Melanie, but still keeping a protective hand on my hip.

"How about you? How are you handling everything?"

"Just a little surprised," she answered. "Alton was never my favorite person, but I thought he'd get stabbed in the balls because he hit on the wrong woman or something. I didn't think he was the type of person to kill himself." She rubbed her arms, a chill overtaking her as the ocean breeze wrapped around us.

"Regardless of any of his past misdeeds, I am sorry for your loss." He shifted his gaze toward me. "Both of you."

"Thank you," I said.

"I should hit the road," Melanie interjected, her voice brightening. "It was good seeing you again, Gideon."

"Always a pleasure, Ms. Burnham." He nodded slightly.

"Text me when you get home," I ordered as she reached her car and opened the door.

"I will."

"And if you get tired on the drive, you can always call and I'll keep you awake."

"Remember what I said. Special place in hell." She gave me an exaggerated wink, then slipped behind the wheel, closing the door behind her.

"Special place in hell?" Gideon asked once her car disappeared down the street.

I fully faced him, draping an arm along his shoulder and toying with a few tendrils of hair that fell over his collar.

"Melanie claims there's a special place in hell for people who interfere with others getting some good dick."

He stared at me for several moments. Then he threw

his head back and laughed, the sound echoing in the night sky.

For a brief moment, as I stood on my front porch with Gideon's arms wrapped around me, everything felt right. This was exactly what I'd needed since overhearing Liam and James' conversation.

Sure, Melanie talked some sense into me, made me realize the chances of Samuel still being alive were nonexistent. But being with Gideon — hearing his laughter and feeling his warmth — it reminded me of what was important.

And it wasn't my past.

"She's quite the character, isn't she?" he remarked with a twinkle in his eye.

"She certainly is. But I wouldn't have it any other way."

He leaned down and brushed a kiss to my forehead. "Either would I."

With a gentle hand on the small of my back, he guided me into my townhouse. As we stepped inside, his sudden stop caught me off guard and I turned to see what had stolen his attention. His eyes were fixated on the box with Samuel's name emblazoned on the outside.

"Should I be concerned?" He blew out a nervous laugh.

"I'm sorry." I rushed toward the coffee table, hastily

gathering up the papers and returning them to the box, securing the lid to it once more.

"Taking a trip down memory lane?"

"It's not that. I just..." I exhaled a deep breath, unsure how to explain this without sounding like I was crazy. "I went over Liam's after I heard about Alton."

"How did that go?" He removed his suit jacket and draped it over the barstool in the kitchen.

The gesture filled me with relief that he wasn't going to leave after walking in and finding a box devoted to my ex.

"It didn't."

"What do you mean?"

"When I was there, I overheard him talk to James about a glass found at Alton's cabin with Samuel's finger-prints on it." I laughed to myself. "For a minute, I was convinced he was still alive."

His eyes widened, and he swallowed hard.

"Thankfully, Melanie made me realize how crazy that was. Samuel's body may never have been found, but every expert who's examined the evidence came to the same conclusion. He wouldn't have survived losing that amount of blood without immediate medical interven-tion. So...I'm sorry."

Approaching me, he grabbed my hand in his, rubbing his thumb along my knuckles in a soothing gesture. "Why are you apologizing to me?"

"I'm trying to stop living in the past, yet every time I'm reminded of it, I cling to it like a life preserver. You don't deserve that."

"If that's what you need, it's okay." He moved his hands to my cheeks. "Like I told you last night...or, I suppose, this morning..." He pushed out a subtle laugh under his breath, the deep chuckle hitting me in places I'd forgotten existed until this man reminded me what it felt like to live again. "Your past made you into the woman you are right now." His mouth inched toward mine, making me breathless from the promise of his kiss. "And I'm crazy about you right here. Right now. Scars and all."

I swallowed hard, staring into his mesmerizing sapphire eyes. If I ignored everything else about him — the crooked nose, high cheekbones, square jawline, well-trimmed facial hair, as well as his perfectly straight teeth — if I only focused on his eyes, *he* could be Samuel.

But that was absurd. Gideon was *not* Samuel. As much as it hurt to admit, Samuel was my past. Gideon could be my future...if I would just finally let go of my past.

Finally let go of Samuel, for once and for all.

With a desperate need to feel grounded in the present, I slammed my mouth against Gideon's, tangling my fingers in his hair and savoring in the silky texture.

Any lingering worry or anxiety from today evaporated as I gave myself over to the moment.

To the present.

I pulled him closer, parting my lips to allow him access, our tongues colliding in a desperate battle as my fingers wrapped around his tie like a lifeline. Hungry for more of him, I fumbled with the knot until it gave way under my insistent hands, eager to explore every inch of him. But as I reached for the top button on his shirt, he grabbed my wrist, preventing me from going any further.

The memory of last weekend flashed through my mind. How he didn't want me to see him shirtless. Exposed. Vulnerable.

I thought we were past that.

Especially after last night when I let him come inside me with no protection.

"What's wrong?" I darted my eyes toward his.

"I don't want you to think the only reason I came over here is to sleep with you. Don't get me wrong," he added with a laugh. "I love fucking you, but that's not why I'm here. I came to check on you. Make sure you were okay. Not because I wanted to get off."

"And I appreciate that," I murmured, dragging my fingers up his chest and toying with the top button of his shirt once more. Then I hoisted myself onto my toes, nibbling on his earlobe. "But I *do* want to get off. I need this, Gideon. Need to forget the past. Need to live in the present."

He held my face in his hands, his conflicted eyes locking with mine, as if torn between two impossible choices. For a moment, I expected him to reveal some earth-shattering truth that would destroy my world worse than the idea of Samuel Tate still being alive ever could.

Then he moved a hand to my hip and tugged me against him, not a breath separating us.

"I'll *always* give you everything you want."

I didn't have a chance to utter another syllable before he crushed his mouth to mine, his kiss erasing all thoughts of my past from my brain.

Because right now, right here, all I cared about was Gideon.

All I *saw* was Gideon.

I prayed that would be enough to keep the ghosts at bay.

CHAPTER SIX

Imogene

I stared at the ceiling, unable to quiet my mind long enough to fall asleep. I shouldn't have had any trouble sleeping. Normally, whenever I spent the night with Gideon, my body was too exhausted, sleep coming easily.

But despite his ravenous appetite for me tonight, I couldn't stop my brain from spinning.

Couldn't stop thinking about that damn glass.

Couldn't stop thinking about Samuel.

It was as if my brain was trying to tell me something. But what?

Discreetly slipping out of bed, I padded out of my room and down the stairs, using my phone to light the way to the kitchen. I opened one of the cabinets and retrieved a glass, filling it with water. As I drank, I leaned against the counter, my gaze fixated on Samuel's name scrawled on the Banker's box.

I could hear Melanie's voice in my head, urging me to move on from the past and focus on my future. Maybe this box was the reason I couldn't sleep, the contents stirring up old emotions and painful memories that were better left forgotten.

Determined, I set my glass on the counter and grabbed a trash bag from under the sink. Then I proceeded to dump the contents of the box into it. After tying the bag tightly, I carried it out to the back deck, dropping it onto the surface with a satisfying thud.

For years, Samuel's ghost had been a constant presence in my life. Now that I was finally taking a step toward moving on from my past, I felt lighter, a weight lifting off my shoulders.

But I'd never be completely free when traces of Samuel's memory still lingered in every inch of my home. It was time to let go of these reminders. I'd never forget him entirely, but I needed to stop surrounding myself with memories that continued to hold me hostage. Otherwise, I'd forever be trapped in a vicious cycle of taking one step forward, then three steps back.

Making my way into my office, I went through all my framed photographs adorning the bookshelves, removing any that included Samuel and placing them in the now empty Banker's box. It wasn't until I reached a photo of Samuel, Ollie, and me that I hesitated. All the other photos were group shots of Melanie, Liam, Samuel, and me.

But this one... This was special. It captured a moment when I was truly happy. I studied the photo of Samuel and me standing on the beach with Ollie between us. I could physically see how happy we were. Could physically *feel* the love we had for each other.

We shared something so special. But like Gideon told me last night. What I shared with Samuel helped me become the woman I was today. And he was falling for *that* woman. As much as I missed Samuel, I needed to let go of him.

Resolved, I placed the framed photo on top of the others, pausing when something in it caught my attention. A birthmark near Samuel's hipbone.

Grabbing it once more, I squinted, studying the imperfection I'd forgotten about over the years. It was similar to the one Gideon had in the same spot. But it wasn't the same shape.

Then again, maybe that was simply due to the scars marring his skin.

What was I even thinking? That Gideon was Samuel?

It was absurd. They were two completely different

people. Not to mention Gideon looked nothing like Samuel.

Yet I still grabbed my phone and navigated toward the album containing all the photos and videos I'd avoided for years. This was the last thing I should have been doing, considering I'd just vowed to stop dwelling on the past.

I rationalized my actions by telling myself that once I found a clearer photo or video of Samuel, proving the birthmark in no way resembled Gideon's, I'd finally let go and move on.

As I scrolled through hundreds of photos and videos, my eyes lingered on one video in particular. It had been taken around the same time as the photo in question and captured Samuel and Ollie playing together on the beach.

The sun shone brightly in the brilliant blue sky, casting a warm glow over them. Samuel threw a tennis ball toward the ocean, his laughter ringing out as Ollie eagerly dove into the shallow water to retrieve it, his furry body glistening with droplets of saltwater upon resurfacing.

But Ollie could never play fetch with just one ball. Instead, whenever he ran back to Samuel, he refused to let go of the ball in his mouth until Samuel produced a second one. Only then would Ollie drop the ball, anxiously waiting for Samuel to throw the new one.

My heart warmed as I watched Samuel and Ollie play together, swiping through more videos I'd taken that day. In one of them, Ollie had just retrieved his ball from the water when a seagull landed nearby. He immediately dropped the ball and chased after the seagull instead.

Without missing a beat, Samuel bellowed, "Ollie, heel!"

The sound of his voice caused me to suck in a sharp intake of air.

But it wasn't just his voice. It was *that* voice. Those words. That command.

It was practically identical to the way Gideon sounded when he ordered Ollie to heel the other day.

As I replayed the video and listened to Samuel repeat the same command, he sounded more and more like Gideon.

Or maybe I simply *wanted* him to sound more and more like Gideon.

I couldn't be sure.

All I did know was I thought there was something familiar about him from the beginning. Now, as I watched old videos of Samuel, that feeling only grew stronger.

I dug my fingers into my hair, feeling like I was on a constant seesaw with no way of getting off. I reminded myself of what Melanie said earlier. That if Samuel *were* still alive, he wouldn't have stayed away from me. Plus, every medical expert insisted he couldn't have survived after losing that much blood. Samuel Tate was dead.

That still didn't stop me from analyzing everything about Samuel in the videos. From the way he moved. To the way he laughed. To the smooth cadence of his voice.

If I closed my eyes, it could have been Gideon.

But how could that be?

I continued to scroll through all the photos and videos, searching for one of Samuel without his shirt on. When I landed on one I'd taken as he lay by the pool, I clicked on it.

His features were softer than Gideon's, his jaw smoother, nose smaller, face thinner. But those piercing eyes and strong brow were unmistakably the same. I moved down the photo to analyze the rest of his body.

The body I once knew so intimately but now seemed almost foreign to me after all this time.

While Samuel was in amazing shape from years of wrestling and martial arts, he wasn't as bulky as Gideon. Regardless of the differences, I zoomed in on his torso, scrutinizing every mark and blemish.

It was one thing for him to have a similar birthmark.

It was another to also have an identical scar right below the ribcage from where one of Samuel's foster brothers burned him with a cigarette. A scar I'd forgotten about until now.

In all the times I'd seen Gideon without a shirt on, it

hadn't even dawned on me that Samuel had a similar scar. In my defense, my mind was typically preoccupied whenever I saw Gideon shirtless.

Now, the similarity was glaring at me.

Not even thinking about what I was doing, I stormed up the stairs and burst into my bedroom. Crawling onto the bed, I yanked the duvet down Gideon's body, revealing his heavily scarred torso. Red lines crisscrossed his skin, some deep and jagged, while others were only a subtle reminder of his past.

And amongst the many scars were the same cigarette burns and birthmark Samuel had in this photo, although Gideon's were duller and his birthmark wasn't quite the same shape, having been cut off by one of his scars.

Still, they were in the same exact spot as Samuel.

That couldn't be a coincidence.

"Ready to go again?" Gideon asked, his voice raspy as he opened his eyes to meet my gaze.

"How did you get this?" I demanded, pointing to the burns in question.

"What do you—"

"These marks right here." I ran my fingers along them, a thousand memories of doing the same thing with Samuel flooding back. "How did you get them?" I barely squeaked out.

He hesitated, his expression shifting from confusion

to something resembling dread. "I told you. I was in a car accident."

"I know what you told me," I snapped, my eyes on fire as I leaned closer. "How did you *really* get them?"

His Adam's apple bobbed up and down in a nervous swallow as he shifted his gaze to meet mine. "What's this all about?"

I tried to remember what Melanie's father once said about how to tell if someone was lying or hoping to deceive you. I thought he mentioned something about eye contact. That if someone failed to look you directly in the eye, it was a surefire way to know they were lying.

As was trying to be evasive when answering.

While Gideon's eye contact remained steady, he *was* being evasive.

"Tell me how you got these marks," I ordered, although my voice quivered with emotion over the idea that Gideon *was* Samuel and he'd been lying to me all along.

Or was I just so desperate to have Samuel back that I was willing to accuse a man who had done nothing but show a sincere interest in me of being my dead boyfriend?

It sounded so crazy. But I couldn't ignore the nagging feeling in my gut that had been there since the first time I saw Gideon.

"Are you Samuel Tate?" I somehow managed to

choke out as I showed him the zoomed-in image of the cigarette burns on Samuel's body.

His brow furrowed, deepening the lines of worry etched on his face as he looked between me and my phone. For a moment, I thought I saw a flicker of panic in his expression, like an animal caught in a trap. But as he returned his eyes to mine, there was nothing but heartache and pain within.

"You think I'm your ex?" His voice was strained, evidencing how much my line of questioning hurt him. "Or perhaps that's who you *want* me to be."

He jumped out of the bed, his body coiled and tense. With swift and determined movements, he angrily yanked on his boxer briefs before stepping into his pants.

"I'm sorry to disappoint you, Imogene, but I'm *not* him. I just..." He pinched his lips together into a tight line as he dug his fingers through his hair in frustration. When he finally looked at me again, defeat swirled in his blue eyes.

"I care about you, Imogene. More than I ever thought I would. I'm trying so damn hard to be understanding of your past, but this..." He shook his head as he tugged on his shirt, leaving it unbuttoned. His stare held a mixture of sadness and pity as it met mine. "I want to be with someone who wants to be with me." He gestured down his torso. "Scars and all. Not with someone who wishes I were someone else."

He abruptly spun on his heels and stormed out of the bedroom, his footfalls heavy as he made his way out of my townhouse. The door slammed shut behind him, the reverberations filling the sudden silence that now surrounded me.

Several seconds ticked by as I stared into space, listening as his car hummed to life outside.

Every fiber of my being screamed for me to chase after him. To apologize and beg for forgiveness. Explain I was just confused by everything I'd learned over the past few hours.

But something held me back, an invisible force keeping me frozen in place.

So instead of going after him and apologizing for my irrational behavior, I collapsed onto my bed, my only company that of my dog and the lingering presence of Samuel's ghost that I feared would haunt me for the rest of my days.

CHAPTER SEVEN

Gideon

I killed the ignition on my Jaguar, but didn't make any move to get out, my gaze fixated on the shoreline in the distance. The sun had just begun to rise behind the mountains, casting a glow over the surfers bobbing up and down on the ocean waves.

Was Imogene out there?

I needed to stop thinking about her.

Obsessing over her.

Tonight confirmed everything Henry tried to warn me about.

I hated essentially gaslighting her like I did, making her feel like a shitty person for accusing me of being her long-lost love.

Which I was.

But like Henry told me, I was in too deep. It was only a matter of time before she learned the truth. She was already suspicious. I needed to either come clean or walk away.

I needed to choose between revenge or love.

I chose revenge.

Until James and Liam paid for their sins, I would always choose revenge. It wasn't even a choice, though. I was a slave to my revenge. It was my master and I was merely a puppet, allowing this desperate need to control me.

To *consume* me.

It didn't make walking away from Imogene any easier, though, even if I knew it was for the best. Which was why I'd spent the past few hours driving aimlessly around San Diego, trying to convince myself I did the right thing.

I'd seen firsthand how much Samuel's death still haunted her. It was selfish of me to pursue something with her when I had no plans for a future. When I was willing to sacrifice myself in order to fulfill my vendetta.

She already lost me once.

I would be a complete asshole if I allowed her to mourn me twice.

With the weight of everything bearing down on me, I opened the door and stepped out of my car. The world was peaceful in the predawn hours, only the faint squawk of seagulls breaking through the sound of the nearby ocean waves.

I slowly made my way up the front steps of my house and slipped inside, expecting it to be quiet.

I should have known better.

As I entered the kitchen, I found Henry by the one-cup brewer, still wearing the same t-shirt and shorts he wore when I left last night.

"Did you sleep in your clothes?" I asked, moving toward him and grabbing a mug from the cabinet.

"That would require sleep."

"You haven't slept?" I arched a brow.

"It doesn't look like you have, either." He gestured to my disheveled appearance, my shirt still unbuttoned and pants crumpled.

"You know I don't sleep well in an actual bed."

After spending four years sleeping on a cold, cement floor, my body had grown accustomed to that. It wasn't until I spent the night with Imogene last weekend that I'd finally found comfort in a real bed again.

Shouldn't that have been enough of a reason for me to realize what was important? To forget about this desperate need for revenge and focus only on the future? I was given a second chance in life. Was I just throwing it away?

"I think it's more than that."

Sometimes I hated how well Henry could read me. It

was why he was the only person I trusted to help me carry out my plan. He could anticipate my needs without me having to say a single word.

And he wasn't afraid to call me out on my bullshit when necessary.

Like he did yesterday.

"I broke things off with her," I finally admitted as I pressed the button on the coffee maker and it whirred to life, the nutty aroma surrounding me.

"You did?" His eyes widened.

"You were right. She doesn't deserve this."

I didn't tell him she figured out the truth, but instead of admitting it, I put the blame on her, making her out to be a woman still in love with a ghost.

I wasn't sure I'd ever be able to confess what I'd done, the guilt still weighing me down. Especially every time I closed my eyes and saw Imogene's bewildered expression in the seconds before I stormed out of her bedroom. Not to mention the hurt in her eyes as she examined my body, finding the same burn marks as Samuel.

As *me*.

"That couldn't have been easy," Henry offered sympathetically. "You care about her, whether as the man you once were or the man you are now. I'm glad you finally saw the harm you'd continue to cause her."

I didn't respond, taking a sip of my coffee and trying to push thoughts of Imogene out of my mind.

"What kept you up all night?" I cleared my throat, needing to change the subject.

He studied me for a beat, but thankfully didn't press any further about Imogene. "Follow me."

He headed out of the kitchen and down the corridor leading to his office, the evidence of his all-nighter scattered on the desk in the form of discarded coffee mugs and dirty dishes.

"Remember how James kept looking at his phone today? Or yesterday," he corrected.

"Sure." I scrunched my brows, wondering why he thought that odd. "I figured he was just searching for any potential public relations backlash over Alton's death."

"I thought so, too. But I never like to assume anything, especially where these assholes are concerned."

"You have a point there."

After all, I'd assumed these men were my friends, only for Liam to stab me in the back.

Or, more accurately, shoot me in my abdomen.

"I did some digging and was able to access James' phone records."

"I'm not sure I want to know how you did that." I laughed under my breath.

It was one thing to access a random citizen's call log. It was another to access that of a United States Senator.

"You don't." His lips turned up into a conniving grin,

reminding me why I was glad to have Henry on my side. "He made about a dozen calls to the same number in half as many hours. And these calls didn't start until he was notified of the somewhat surprising evidence found at Alton's cabin."

"Who was he calling?"

"The number was untraceable, but lucky for us, James has never been a patient man. Or all that smart. After not getting an answer for the tenth or eleventh time, he made another call. This one to a number that *is* traceable. Hell, it's more than just traceable. It's searchable on the internet." He typed on his keyboard, and the webpage for a funeral home in Atlanta popped up.

I stared at it for several long moments, my mind spinning. "Maybe he's planning Alton's memorial. He *did* get his start in Atlanta." I swallowed hard. "We all did."

"That doesn't explain the incessant calls he made whenever Liam was out of the room. Which is why I decided to do some digging."

"I figured you would."

"The owner of this funeral home is a man by the name of Brian McGuire. He's been a licensed funeral director for the past fifteen years. But for the ten years before getting his degree in mortuary science, he worked for a company called Aftermath Cleaning."

His fingers flew over the keyboard once more, and another website popped up on the monitor. But unlike I initially assumed, this wasn't a normal in-home cleaning service. Their specialty was crime scene cleanup.

Why would James be anxious to speak to this funeral director, assuming he was the owner of that untraceable number?

"Is there a picture of this Brian McGuire?"

"Sure." Henry clicked a few buttons and a bio page from the funeral home's website appeared, a photo of a dark-haired man of average build and blue-gray eyes staring back at me. But what caught my attention was the pin on his lapel, a black background with a gold B in elegant script.

A ghost of a memory slammed into me, and I squeezed my eyes shut, placing a hand on the desk to steady myself. I'd seen that pin before. I was sure of it.

"You okay?" Henry asked, his gaze narrowed in concern. "Do you recognize him?"

"I..." I shook my head, blinking repeatedly. "I don't know."

"Well, it appears James is planning on paying McGuire a visit. I was able to access the funeral home's servers and found an email from McGuire to one of his employees instructing her to clear his schedule for tomorrow morning and give the staff the day off due to a VIP client coming in."

"And you're certain this couldn't just be James trying to plan Alton's memorial?"

Henry arched a skeptical brow at my suggestion. "This is a man who had his chief of staff plan his own mother's funeral last year. Do you honestly think he'd put in this much effort?"

"I don't know *what* to believe right now," I answered honestly. "But I don't think we'll get any answers by staying here."

"I couldn't agree more."

CHAPTER EIGHT

Imogene

The rising sun warmed my skin as Ollie jogged in front of me, wearing the same dopey smile on his face that always reminded me of Samuel.

Which now also reminded me of Gideon.

I couldn't sleep after Gideon left. Instead, all I could think about was how devastated he looked when I accused him of being Samuel.

Now that I had time to think about everything, something I didn't do last night, I couldn't help but feel like a complete asshole for what I'd done.

Who did that? Who accused the man they were falling for of being their dead boyfriend?

Apparently, I did.

It was official.

I was losing my mind.

So what if he had burn marks in the same spot? He looked *nothing* like Samuel. That should have been all the proof I needed that he wasn't him. Not to mention, Samuel Tate was dead. Why was it so hard for me to accept that?

My phone buzzed in my pocket, pulling me out of my thoughts as a flicker of hope burned in my chest that it was Gideon. Truthfully, the reason I took Ollie for a walk along the beach this morning was because I secretly hoped I'd run into him like I had so many other times.

And maybe my dog could act as a sort of peace offering, considering how much Gideon adored him.

But he wasn't out here this morning like he had been in the past.

To further my disappointment, when I checked my phone, the text was from my mother instead of Gideon.

MOM:

Just checking to see how you're doing this morning, all things considered. If you need some time away, you're always welcome here.

A heavy sigh escaped my lips as I slid my phone back into my pocket, not ready to respond just yet. Even in texts, she'd know something was wrong. She always did.

Instead, I made my way toward The Daily Grind, securing Ollie's leash to the post by the front door before heading inside.

The barista smiled, already reaching for a medium-sized coffee cup. "Your usual?"

"Yes, please."

"You got it." Spinning, she headed toward the espresso machine, pressing a few buttons to make it whir to life. "It looks like he finally got the nerve to ask you out," she remarked as she worked.

"What's that?"

She playfully waggled her brows. "Mr. Tall, Dark, and Mysterious. At least that's what I named him. I saw him walking Ollie yesterday morning." She nodded toward the large front windows, my dog looking inside in anticipation of me bringing him a pup cup. "I assume it's because he finally asked you out."

"He did." I forced a smile, in no mood to delve into the details of my current relationship status with Mr. Tall, Dark, and Mysterious, as she called him.

"It's about time," she exhaled. "That man has been sitting outside every morning just waiting for you to either run by or go surfing."

"What?" I blinked repeatedly, her statement catching me off guard.

While I saw him out here a few times myself, I

thought it was merely a coincidence. Could it have been more than that?

Liam raised his concerns last weekend. Thought it was odd Gideon just so happened to be at the club when I was attacked. And then the body of the man who'd been giving me those necklaces was uncovered on Liam's boat. Not to mention, Alton used information he'd supposedly seen on Gideon's desk to make a bunch of bad trades, which cost him millions. And his life. Sure, it was illegal, but did Gideon intentionally leave bogus information out, as Liam insisted?

"Not like a stalker or anything," she quickly corrected, probably noticing my expression turning pale. "I just thought it was...refreshing. Most people barely look up from their phones. Not him." She chuckled under her breath as she added hot water to the espresso. "In fact, I don't think I've ever seen him look at his phone. Instead, he always bought an actual newspaper instead of reading the news online. You don't see a lot of that these days."

"When did you first notice him?" I asked guardedly, my mind reeling.

She pinched her lips together as she tapped her fingernails against the counter. "Probably around the same time you starting coming here." She shifted her gaze to me. "Come to think of it, I'm almost certain it was the same day." Her expression brightened. "If that's not fate, I don't know what is."

After adding a bit of steamed milk to my beverage, she handed it to me. I mindlessly gave her some cash, telling her to keep the change, then turned.

Was Liam right? Was there more to Gideon's interest in me than he'd led me to believe?

Or was I just allowing Liam to manipulate me?

After I lost Samuel, I swore I'd never let him come between me and someone I cared about.

Was I repeating the past all over again?

"Wait!" the barista called out just as I was about to open the door. "Can't forget about my man out there." She sprayed some whipped cream into a tiny cup and skirted out from behind the counter to hand it to me.

"Thanks," I mumbled, then slipped outside, Ollie jumping on me the second he saw the treat in my hands.

The walk back to the townhouse was a complete blur. My mind was consumed with thoughts of Gideon, how he'd been watching me for weeks before I noticed him. Why? What game was he playing? Or maybe it wasn't a game at all. Maybe it was just a twist of fate, like the barista said. Maybe he noticed me and kept returning in the hopes of seeing me again.

I swooned over that kind of thing in romance novels.

Why did I struggle to believe it could happen in real life?

Because my life had always been more like a psychological thriller than a romantic comedy.

One thing was certain. I needed a break from the constant seesaw my emotions had been on since learning about that damn glass yesterday.

And I knew exactly where to find the clarity I desperately needed.

CHAPTER NINE

Gideon

"You okay?" Henry asked as he pulled the SUV to a stop a block away from a Victorian house in the Buckhead area of Atlanta.

An uneasy sense of déjà vu filled me as I studied the old building. There was something familiar about the turrets and wrap-around porch. Not to mention the sign out front with Buckhead Funeral Home on it, the elaborate B styled in the same way as the pin Brian McGuire wore in his website photo.

This place made my skin crawl, and Henry knew it.

"Yeah. Fine."

I gave him a reassuring smile, trying to downplay the knot building in my stomach. I couldn't lose focus now. Not when my gut told me there was a damn good reason

James Turner flew all the way out here, and it had nothing to do with planning Alton's memorial service.

"Looks like it's showtime," I announced when a sleek, dark sedan passed by, much to my relief.

Henry shifted his attention away from me as the car turned into the public lot across the street that was shared by several other area businesses — coffee shops, boutique clothing stores, even a bakery.

Clicking a button on his comm unit, Henry announced, "He's parking now."

I grabbed a small pair of binoculars and held them up to my eyes, watching James get out of the sedan, wearing casual clothes along with a baseball cap.

Which only increased my suspicion that something was going on. I couldn't remember the last time I'd seen him dressed so casually. I didn't think he owned anything other than designer suits and top-of-the-line golf attire.

As he hurried along the sidewalk, his attention remained glued to his phone, causing him to bump into a man jogging past him. Without missing a beat, James berated him.

The runner gave an apologetic smile, then continued down the sidewalk while James returned his attention to his phone.

"It's done," a voice crackled over Henry's laptop.

"Copy," Henry responded.

"What's done?" I asked.

He gestured toward the runner. "I had one of my guys slip a tiny microphone into his pocket in case they meet somewhere I can't access." He hit a few keys on his laptop, bringing up a security feed of the funeral home.

The second he did, another wave of déjà vu slammed into me, this time leaving me momentarily breathless. Especially when I saw a few of the preparation rooms. More memories flashed before my eyes, but as had been the case for years, they were too foggy and jumbled for me to make much sense of with any certainty. But something about that sterile, windowless room stirred something loose in my memory. It wasn't that exact room, but I remember waking up in a room just like it after the man I thought to be a good Samaritan came to my rescue as I bled out in my car.

"You okay?" Henry studied me, his concern increasing with every second.

"Fine. I just... Being back in Atlanta again is bringing up some memories."

I fully expected him to call me out on my bullshit, but before he could, there was a motion on one of the feeds. A man walked down a long hallway and opened the front door.

"Senator Turner," he greeted James with a handshake as he entered the foyer. "It's good to see you again, although I'm sorry it's not under better circumstances."

I leaned closer, analyzing every detail about the two

men. Their words. Their tone. Their body language. Anything that could provide a clue about what was going on.

But there was nothing.

"You and me both, Mr. McGuire." James forced a sad smile, playing the part of the bereaved friend. Much like he did in the video clips I saw of him after my supposed passing. "Is there somewhere we can talk in private? As I mentioned, there's a very pressing matter I need to discuss with you."

"Certainly. This way, please." Brian spun around and walked down the hallway with an air of confidence.

What was James' connection to him?

And why did I sense Brian had the upper hand?

"I worried this might happen," Henry remarked when the two men disappeared from view.

"What's that?"

"That they'd talk in Brian's private office. It's one of the few rooms not wired into the security system. And since we're short on time, I wasn't able to break in and install anything."

"What other rooms aren't wired?" I asked out of curiosity.

"It's hard to know for certain. I was able to pull a blueprint from when he bought this house, since he had to submit plans for the remodel. From what I can tell, all the first floor rooms are wired. There's the viewing room. The parlor. Arrangement room, as well as several prep rooms. All the administrative offices on the second floor are also wired, apart from his office. The only other place that isn't wired is the cremation room."

"Cremation room?"

"He put an addition on the back of the house, probably because those ovens require some heavy duty walls and insulation."

I nodded as another memory clawed its way to the surface. But like before, it remained just out of reach.

"How can I be of service to you today?" a voice sounded over Henry's laptop, and he turned up the volume.

"Looks like the microphone I planted works," he remarked, but I quickly hushed him. Not because I was interested in the substance of the conversation, although I certainly was.

But there was something familiar about that voice, especially now that it wasn't distorted like on the security feed.

"It was my understanding after our last meeting that our business together was concluded," Brian continued, his tone professional, yet displeased at the same time.

"That was *my* understanding, too," James replied. "Based on *your* assurances."

"I fulfilled my part of the bargain. Made you quite a

bit of money, too, if memory serves. Which is why I was surprised to get your call. *All* of them."

"It's come to my attention that you may not have held up your end of the deal like you led me to believe."

"What do you mean?" I could hear the confusion in Brian's voice.

"Fingerprints belonging to Samuel Tate were found as recent as two days ago," James hissed.

A heavy silence fell over the speaker, broken only by the distant sound of passing cars. What I wouldn't have given to be in that room, to see this guy's expression.

To see *both* of their expressions.

Finally, Brian broke the silence. "I don't see how that has anything to do with me."

"You don't?" James barked out around an incredulous laugh. "It has *everything* to do with you. I hired you to do a simple cleanup job."

"As I'm sure you recall, it wasn't exactly the simple cleanup job we'd originally agreed upon. Not when your friend failed to actually *complete* the job. Like I told you back then. I'm a cleaner. *Not* a killer. I'll dispose of any bodies brought to me, but that's where I draw the line."

I could feel Henry's eyes studying me as I stared at the laptop, as if that would have helped me understand all this better. "Are they talking about—"

I silenced him with another hush, my heart pounding in my chest.

"I gave you an option. One that paid you handsomely."

"Except Samuel Tate's goddamn fingerprints were found!" James reminded him yet again. "By the fucking cops when they were investigating Alton Sinclair's death! You promised you'd make him disappear and none of the evidence you left behind would ever be tied to us."

"And that's precisely what I did. Last I checked, some kid was arrested for the murder, who then tragically lost his life during a prison fight. Case closed."

"Not if Samuel's DNA has been found recently. You swore that, even if he somehow managed to survive any length of time, he'd never be able to escape."

"No. I simply said the probability of him surviving any length of time was *extremely* low. Need I remind you again that this was your decision? And the money you made off the deal allowed you to run for and win the senate race."

"You made money off the deal, too."

"Merely a cut for putting you in touch with my contact," Brian retorted with a hint of amusement. "If you're upset with the outcome, take it up with him. Although I don't think he'll be as...forgiving as I am. From what I hear, he's more the type of person to shoot first and ask questions later."

"Aren't you worried what this could mean?" James

seethed, his tone dripping with frustration. "If the police reopen the investigation into Samuel Tate's death, they might learn of your involvement."

"They'd only learn about that if *you* tell them about it. And I know you're not that stupid. *Are* you? Because I'd hate for you to have a taste of what poor Samuel Tate had to suffer."

"You wouldn't."

"Try me," Brian responded with pure venom, the room falling eerily silent. Then he cleared his throat, his tone becoming professional once more. "I trust you can find your way out."

Silence hung heavy in the air, punctured only by my ragged breaths and the thunderous racing of my heart. I pictured both men glaring at each other, willing the other to make the first move.

Finally, I heard what sounded like the rustling of clothes, followed by faint footsteps. A few seconds later, James emerged from the funeral home.

Just the sight of him filled me with rage, my jaw ticking as I repeatedly clenched and unclenched my fists.

"Don't." Henry touched a hand to my forearm. "Not now. Not without a plan."

But I couldn't let it go. Not after everything I just learned. The betrayal. The deceit. The utter disregard for human life.

For *my* life.

I'd always planned on eliminating James after what he did to Jonah. I thought that was the extent of his involvement. Thought it was just bad luck that the man who found me had ill intentions.

I never could have imagined James not only hired him to clean up Liam's mess but also conspired to sell me like I was merely a piece of property. Not a man he considered a friend.

All to increase his wealth.

I turned my fiery gaze upon the Victorian house. When Brian McGuire appeared in the second-floor window, my blood boiled, my anger growing with every passing second.

"There's someone else I need to add to my list," I ground out.

Henry gave a resigned nod. "I had a feeling you were going to say that."

CHAPTER TEN

Imogene

Artificial light shone brightly overhead as I made my way through the bustling crowd of Atlanta airport on Sunday morning after a restless red-eye flight. When I finally emerged from the secure area, my tired body was instantly enveloped in a sense of peace, and I couldn't deny the relief of being back in a familiar place.

I could only hope this break would give me the clarity I needed.

Or that my mother would talk some sense into me. She was always good at that.

As I pulled up the rideshare app on my phone, a few excited voices sounded from behind me.

"Is that Lachlan Hale?"

I snapped my head up, coming to an abrupt stop

when I saw my step-father signing autographs for eager fans a few feet away. Even though it had been years since he'd played professional baseball, people still recognized him, especially in Atlanta. He was a legend around here.

As he handed a hat back to a little boy who couldn't have been more than six, he caught sight of me. He politely excused himself, offering his apologies, then headed in my direction.

"Hey, kid," he greeted in his familiar Australian accent.

While it was much more Americanized than when I first met him fifteen years ago, it was still there. I hoped it always would be. It reminded me of home. Of family.

"You didn't have to come get me," I told him as he pulled me into his chest, kissing the top of my head. "I would have taken an Uber."

"Your mother worries about you enough as it is. Letting you get in the car with a stranger you book on the internet?"

I rolled my eyes at his overprotective nature, especially considering I was now in my thirties. In his eyes, I'd always be the awkward teenager he once bribed with pancakes in order to win me over and let him date my mother.

"I'd rather stay on her good side." With a wink and a smile, he reached for the handle of my roll-aboard. "Let me get that for you."

"Thanks."

"Anytime, kid." With a playful nudge, he steered me toward the airport exit, waving at a few people who recognized him as we passed.

The second we stepped through the sliding glass doors, a wall of humidity assaulted me, even at nine in the morning. I could already feel my hair curling despite straightening it yesterday.

"I bet you don't miss this weather, do you?"

"Actually, I do." I inhaled a deep breath. "Don't get me wrong. I love California and don't miss running in this kind of humidity, but there are quite a few things about Atlanta I miss."

"Like a Varsity dog?" he asked, referencing the famous Atlanta spot he often took me during my teen years whenever he picked me up from school.

"*Definitely* a Varsity dog." I laughed, following him into the parking garage, the two of us falling into a comfortable silence as he led me toward his SUV, the scent of exhaust and wet concrete heavy in the air.

"How are things with Gideon?" Lachlan asked once we were on the freeway toward the house he shared with my mother. Even though it was Sunday, there was still quite a bit of traffic. Thankfully, I was used to it. "Is he treating you right?"

"Of course." I plastered a fake smile on my face, praying he couldn't see through my lies.

What was I going to tell him? That the reason I took an impromptu trip home was because I'd just accused him of being Samuel and was now questioning everything?

That, after finding a photo of Samuel with the same burns and birthmark, I'd been so convinced he *was* Samuel.

That I felt like an ass when he accused me of only being with him because I wished he was my dead boyfriend.

That I was certain I'd overreacted until I learned he'd been watching me for weeks before I approached him outside The Daily Grind.

That I still didn't know what to think.

One second, I was convinced I was letting Liam manipulate me into thinking the worst of Gideon. The next, I couldn't help but feel like there were too many coincidences for everything to simply be a series of unrelated events.

Or fate.

Which was why I needed to get out of California, even if only for a few days. I needed to get off this emotional seesaw that had me constantly second-guessing everything. Needed to be somewhere without any reminders of Gideon, even if I'd be surrounded by countless memories of Samuel.

Maybe that was what I needed, though.

"He better be," Lachlan replied sternly. "If he doesn't, you let me know and I'll be on the next flight out. So will Nikko."

"Pretty sure that would have him pissing his pants."

Lachlan's cousin, Nikko, was a two-hundred-plus pound Samoan MMA fighter. To say he was huge would have been an understatement. Lachlan was a pretty big guy. He'd have to be in order to play professional baseball like he did. Next to Nikko, though, he looked like a toothpick.

No doubt Gideon would, too.

"That's the point." Lachlan winked, giving me a conniving grin before returning his attention to the road. "But seriously, Imogene. He better treat you right."

"He's the perfect gentleman."

It wasn't a lie. Gideon *was* the perfect gentleman.

Although I had a feeling Lachlan may not consider Gideon choking me as he fucked me all that gentlemanly.

But I wasn't about to go into detail about my sex life with my step-father.

"Then I'm happy for you." He reached across the center console and grabbed my hand. "After everything you've been through the past few years, you deserve it."

"Thanks."

He gave my hand one last squeeze, then returned it to the steering wheel.

Thankfully, he didn't mention Gideon again during the thirty-minute car ride to the Chastain Park section of Atlanta. Instead, we kept our conversation relatively light. He asked about Ollie and how I liked working for the soccer team. I asked how retirement was treating him. Although it was hard to consider him retired, since he was often asked to commentate, especially for some of the bigger games toward the end of the season. Between that and his numerous charities, he kept himself busy.

"I was actually hoping to talk to you about something, but I didn't want to do it last weekend, since I know how difficult it must have been for you," he said as he drove the familiar streets leading up to his house.

It reminded me of the time I rode my bike all the way out here from my mom's house in Brookhaven after they'd gotten into an argument and I decided to act as a mediator between them.

I knew my mom would never have let me come on my own. Lachlan was pissed, too. I wasn't used to that. Wasn't used to having a father figure in my life. That was the moment I knew he was perfect for my mom. And after I helped him win her back, he forgave me for recklessly putting my life at risk.

"What's that?" I glanced his way.

"My charity is planning to build another ball field here in Atlanta in order to expand the program. Make it even bigger. I'd like to name the field in Samuel's memory. I know Liam kept his charity going in his honor, but I wanted to do something, too, considering all the hours he volunteered for my organization while also running his own."

"He'd like that," I said without hesitation. "He loved giving back to the community whenever he could. And he definitely loved baseball." A subtle laugh escaped my throat. "I'll never forget the look on his face when he realized you were my step-father."

"He was always good to you."

"Yes, he was."

Swallowing hard, I shifted my attention out the window, watching all the familiar houses pass by.

"I'm glad you've found someone who treats you just as good as Samuel."

"Me, too." I managed a small smile, pushing away the nagging thought that maybe it was because Gideon *was* Samuel.

"Come on," Lachlan said once he pulled his car into the massive garage attached to an even more massive house. "Your mum has been baking up a storm."

"Please tell me she didn't stay up all night baking because of me," I groaned as I opened the door and stepped out of the car.

"Not *all* night." He opened the trunk and grabbed my suitcase, meeting me by my door. "You know how she is. She loves to spoil people with food."

"That she does."

I followed him toward the door leading into the house, and he held it open, allowing me to walk in front of him.

"We're home," he called out, his voice echoing against the high ceiling and pristine hardwood floors.

The aroma of sugar and vanilla surrounded me, reminding me of home. Even when my mother wasn't baking, the scent still seemed to cling to the air.

"I'm so glad you're here," my mom said as she rounded the corner from the kitchen, wrapping me in a tight hug before pulling back, her eyes scanning over me in the way only a mother could. "How are you? Are you all right? How are Liam and James?"

"As good as can be expected."

"I didn't even care for Alton that much, but I never would have wished anything like this on him."

"Me, neither."

"Will you give Liam our condolences the next time you speak to him?"

"Of course." I gritted a smile, not wanting to tell her I hadn't spoken to Liam in over a week. That we'd gotten into an argument over Gideon and now I was questioning whether Liam may have been right about him after all.

"Are you hungry? I made some danishes and muffins. Or I can whip up some eggs or a frittata."

"Honestly, I'm more tired than anything right now," I admitted around a yawn.

"Why don't you go upstairs and rest? Then maybe tonight we can have a girl's night. Go have some drinks and catch up without any distractions."

I sighed, tension rolling off my shoulders. A night out with my mother was exactly what I needed.

"I'd like that."

"Good." She gave me another hug and pressed a gentle kiss to my forehead. "If you need anything, let me know."

I turned from her, climbing the familiar stairs to my old bedroom, not surprised to see that Lachlan had already dropped off my suitcase. Exhaustion settled in my bones, and I collapsed onto the bed, relishing in the feel of the soft duvet against my skin.

But despite having barely slept more than a few hours over the past several days, I still couldn't quiet my mind enough to fall asleep.

CHAPTER ELEVEN

Gideon

"You're certain you want to do this tonight?" Henry asked as we sat in the SUV outside the funeral home on Sunday evening. "We haven't had time to prepare. Not like we did with Alton."

"You said it yourself. The more time that lapses between James' visit this morning and what I'm about to do, the less likely the police will consider him a person of interest. You've done more than enough research. I have an opportunity tonight, especially with him giving his staff the day off. I'm going to take it. I *have* to take it."

"There are still a lot of unanswered questions," Henry reminded me. "I tried to run a proper background check on this guy, but there's only so much I can find out in a short period of time. Based on what we overheard earlier, he's definitely involved in more than just cleaning crime scenes. I haven't been able to figure out what that is yet."

"You'll have eyes and ears on me?"

"I've highjacked his feed so it's on a loop, but I'll be able to keep track of you everywhere inside, except for his office and the cremation room."

"Good." I reached for the door handle, but before I could slip into the night, Henry stopped me with a hand on my forearm. I met his green eyes.

"Be careful," he admonished.

"I always am."

He nodded, but didn't let go right away, as if wanting to tell me something else.

"I'll be fine," I assured him.

He closed his eyes and pushed out a long breath. Then he released his hold on me, although I could sense his reluctance.

Smoothing a hand down my suit, I climbed out of the SUV and took a moment to become the person I needed in order to lull Brian McGuire into a false sense of security.

Then again, the money Henry promised when he called to beg for a last-minute meeting for his wealthy boss was probably all Brian cared about. Henry may not have had time to thoroughly research my unexpected target, but he learned enough to know Brian wouldn't be able to turn down a huge pile of money, even if it ended up being detrimental to him.

Which it would.

"You must be Mr. Saint," Brian greeted with a slick smile, opening the door before I even had a chance to ring the doorbell.

Using my name was a risk, but Henry thought it might work to my advantage, considering it would only take a quick internet search for Brian to see my vast wealth.

"Thank you for agreeing to meet with me. I apologize for all the secrecy, but I'm trying to make a plan for my grandfather without the entire world learning his health is failing."

"In my line of work, discretion is of the utmost importance." He stepped aside to let me enter, the familiar smell of roses and clean linen nearly causing me to lose my balance.

"I trust my assistant has compensated you for your time." My tone was smooth and polite, although the longer I remained in this man's presence, the more I wanted to make him suffer. But I kept my cool, reminding myself to be patient.

I'd have my chance to make him suffer before the night was over.

"He has. Thank you."

"It's the least I could do."

"Shall we begin in the viewing room?" Brian extended his arm down the long hallway.

"Certainly." I followed him out of the foyer, my surroundings all muted grays with subtle accents of blue. It was a calming environment in which to say farewell to your loved one.

Or to hold a man hostage before selling him to an underground fighting ring.

"While we have enough space to host large families, if this isn't sufficient, I have contacts at several event spaces in the area and can arrange to host the viewing there instead. I find most of my clients prefer the 'homey' feel this space provides, and they often alter their plans accordingly, opting for a more private viewing before the public service."

"I can see why," I responded, taking note of the spacious room in the back of the house. It could easily fit several dozen mourners.

"Since I understand how difficult this time can be, I also have a separate room just for immediate family." He headed toward a pair of pocket doors on the far wall, sliding them open to reveal another room decorated in the same distinguished style, but on a smaller scale. "We partner with area restaurants to provide refreshments for the family for the duration of the viewing."

"That's a nice touch. I haven't come across many funeral homes that offer that."

"We like to make sure all our guests' needs are taken care of while they're with us."

I made a show of examining both the family space as well as the viewing room before turning back to him. "May I see the preparation rooms?"

He hesitated, his fake smile faltering. "Those aren't typically open to the public."

"I understand, but my grandfather has been quite particular about his final wishes. I want to ensure they can be carried out with dignity."

He shifted uncomfortably from foot to foot, stealing a discreet glance toward a door on the opposite side of the viewing room. I couldn't lose him now. My plan hinged on him going along with my wishes.

"Otherwise, I'll be on my way," I said politely as I started toward the hallway.

"No need," he responded quickly, stepping in front of me. "I've been in this business long enough to understand some people may have different requirements than others. I do have an open preparation room I can show you."

My lips curved up in the corners. "I appreciate that."

I followed him through the viewing room and toward the door he'd just glanced at. He input a code into a numbered lock, and the door buzzed open, revealing a stark, white corridor that felt more like a hospital than a funeral home.

My senses were on high alert as I tried to absorb each detail, everything about my surroundings so damn familiar. The hum of the air conditioning. The buzz from the fluorescent lights overhead. The smell of cleaning supplies. There was no doubt I'd been kept here all those years ago, especially when Brian brought me into one of the rooms, the aroma of antiseptic and bleach so strong I had to swallow down the bile rising in my throat.

I may not have had many clear memories of the time between Liam shooting me and waking up in a cold cell, but certain smells stayed with me.

And this smell would be permanently etched into my memory — an olfactory stamp that would never fade.

"As you can see, we keep our prep rooms clean and sanitized," Brian's voice sliced through my thoughts, his words dripping with faux professionalism. "When the deceased comes to us, we take care to remove all clothes and jewelry and return them to the family, ensuring everything is logged in and out. The last thing we want is for anything of importance to go missing."

"Can you tell me a bit about the embalming process?" I asked in an effort to prevent myself from tackling him to the floor and beating him to death right now.

A gentle smile tugged on his lips. "That's probably

one of the most frequently asked questions. I assure you, it's done with the utmost respect and dignity."

"I don't doubt that, but I was wondering if you could tell me what it entails. I've always been fascinated by this sort of thing, especially after reading a book about how they preserved Lincoln's body."

"Ah, yes. I hear that quite a lot. While the science has definitely improved since the Civil War, the concept is still the same, for the most part. I start by making a few incisions. One to the carotid artery and another to the jugular vein." He gestured to the corresponding parts on his body. "A tube containing embalming fluid is placed by the carotid to pump the mixture through the body while the incision to the jugular acts as a drain, ridding the body of blood. After that, I embalm the cavity."

"The cavity?"

"To preserve the organs. A small incision is placed just above the navel and I place a trocar inside the abdominal and thoracic cavities."

"What's a trocar?"

His smile widened as he headed toward a wall of cabinets on the far side of the room. After sliding open a drawer, he removed what was probably the longest needle I'd ever seen and handed it to me.

"This is a trocar."

"Good thing they're already dead, or you'd put them

off needles for the rest of their lives," I remarked as I studied the instrument with curiosity.

"I almost fainted the first time I used one in school, but I eventually learned to toughen up."

"What do you use this for?" I returned it to him.

"To suction out any remaining blood or bodily fluids before delivering embalming fluid into the organs. After that, all incisions are closed up with sutures."

I nodded, taking a moment to process everything in order to give off an interested impression. In reality, my mind swirled with thoughts of using the trocar on him and sucking all the blood out of his body as he begged for his life.

"My grandfather has mentioned a desire to be cremated instead of buried. Do you still recommend embalming?" I asked finally.

"Even if you decide to go with cremation, embalming helps preserve the body so it looks more...natural during the viewing."

"So less like a corpse?"

"Precisely," he replied with a laugh.

"It's my understanding you have onsite cremation?"

"We do. And I can assure you that no cremations will occur during any visitation or viewing hours. We only do them after business hours."

"May I see the facilities?"

I could sense his reluctance once more. This time,

however, he didn't object to my request. After all, I'd paid him handsomely just to meet with me. No doubt he was already seeing dollar signs in his eyes over what I'd pay to have the perfect service for my nonexistent grandfather.

"Right this way." He spun on his heels.

I followed, but not before discreetly grabbing the trocar he left on the embalming table and slipping it into the sleeve of my suit jacket.

"I had this entire wing built as an addition when I bought the house," he explained proudly as he led me down the hallway. "While I strive to give my guests a comforting environment, there's still a clinical element to what I do, as well as building code requirements in order to carry out cremations on site. I pride myself on being able to offer a one-stop shop service to my clients."

"It certainly is convenient," I mused, although I was thinking more of the convenience it offered for my plans tonight.

After passing several more rooms, he came to a stop at the end of the corridor. Like every other door along this hallway, there was another keypad requiring another code. But in addition, there was also a fingerprint scanner, making me think something more sinister than a typical cremation occurred on the other side of this door.

"Quite a bit of security," I commented as he input his code before pressing his thumb to the scanner.

"As I've mentioned, the safety of your loved one is of my utmost concern."

The door buzzed, and he pushed it open, revealing another sterile space like the preparation room he just showed me.

But this one was much bigger, probably four times the size. And unlike the other room, there was a large oven built into the far wall.

He headed toward a panel beside it and flipped several switches.

When the unmistakable sound of gas igniting filled the room, another memory slammed into me. Something about the beeps and hissing of gas were so familiar, confirming my suspicion that I was kept in one of these sterile rooms as this asshole nursed me back to health, just to turn around and sell me off like livestock.

"How long does a standard cremation typically take?" I asked, needing to distract myself from the rage that was becoming stronger with every second I remained in this place.

"The entire process can take approximately three hours, sometimes longer, depending on the size of the body. The oven is usually preheated to about eleven hundred degrees, which doesn't take long with the powerful flames inside. Once that happens, the mechanized doors are opened and the container is rolled inside before the doors are quickly closed again."

"Container?"

"While it's not necessary, I prefer to keep the body in a combustible container. I find it more...respectful. Sometimes it's just a large cardboard box or simple coffin like this here." His tone was chillingly casual as he walked toward a plywood box in the corner of the room.

"And after the process is complete? What happens to the ashes?"

"The chamber is then cooled and the cremated remains, which actually resemble a skeleton, are swept into a tray. Then the remains are put into this."

He strode toward a machine that looked similar to a tool cabinet, the only difference being the clear doors on the front. He opened them, demonstrating where the remains were placed once they came out of the oven.

"First, the machine will remove any metals, like from fillings or hip or knee replacements. Then it will grind whatever's left." He closed the doors and opened the compartment beneath it, gesturing toward a metal bin where I assumed the grindings ended up. "After that, the remains are placed in a container of the family's choosing, which I personally deliver within forty-eight hours."

Nodding, I strolled through the room, taking in all the equipment, doing my best to remember every detail he just shared with me.

Especially the cremation process.

This asshole probably used this very room to dispose

of bodies and evidence of crimes. Hell, he probably would have used this room to dispose of *my* body had I not still been alive when he arrived at the crime scene that night.

And now I was going to dispose of the evidence of *his* death in an act of poetic justice.

"Well, you've been extremely accommodating and thorough." I faced him with a bright smile. "I can't tell you how much I appreciate you taking the time to go over the entire process with me. It certainly helps make my decision much easier."

"I understand this can be a difficult time. I'm always more than happy to answer any questions you may have."

"I actually do have one more question, if you can spare another minute of your time."

"Certainly." Brian flashed a smile. "Anything to make the decision easier."

In one swift move, I removed the trocar from its hiding spot and plunged it into his stomach.

"How much did you make when you sold me?" I growled, my eyes flaming with fury.

He parted his lips, confusion and panic overtaking his expression. "I don't know what you're talking about," he stammered in a strained voice.

"Then let me refresh your memory." I leaned closer, relishing the fear in his eyes. "Five years ago, you were hired to clean a crime scene. When you arrived, the victim was still alive, so you conspired with a certain soon-to-be United States Senator to make a bit of money. Instead of finishing the job, you brought the victim back here, patched him up, then sold him." My jaw clenched. "Sold *me*."

Recognition flashed in his eyes, his complexion paling even more as he struggled to free himself from my hold. But he was no match for me. After all, I'd spent four years fighting for my life on a regular basis, thanks to him.

I could easily overpower him without even breaking a sweat.

"They said you died. That's why I stopped getting—"

"Getting what?" I roared, twisting the trocar around in his stomach.

A piercing wail ripped through the room as more blood stained his white suit shirt. "A cut," he shouted, his face scrunched up in agony.

I paused my motions. "A cut?"

"It was part of the deal. A finder's fee, so to speak. Any time you won, I got a share of the proceeds. But they told me you died over a year ago."

"They lied," I sneered, removing the trocar from his stomach, his eyes widening in terror in the seconds before I plunged it directly through his heart.

Years ago, this sort of thing would have sickened me.

That was before I became desensitized to death and

torture. Before I had no choice but to live and breathe it every second of every day.

Now I was able to look into the eyes of the man who put me in that hellhole as he struggled for every last gasp of breath until blood sputtered from his mouth and his body went limp.

CHAPTER TWELVE

Imogene

"Now that you've had some rest and it's just us girls," Mom began, twisting her body toward me as we sat at the counter of a trendy bar in Buckhead. "How are things with Gideon?"

The sound of glasses clinking and low chatter filled the air, but since it was a Sunday night, it wasn't too crowded.

"They're good," I lied.

Her lips pressed into a thin line. "Is that *really* the answer you intend to go with, or do you want to take a minute and formulate a different response?"

"What do you mean?" I shifted uncomfortably on my barstool, avoiding her gaze as I took a sip of my old fashioned, savoring in the sharp burn of the bourbon as it warmed my insides.

"As much as I'd love to think this impromptu trip is simply because you miss your mother, I have a feeling something else prompted it. Especially since you've been...off."

"Off? Off how?"

"Don't forget I carried you inside me for nine months. Raised you to be the amazing woman you are. I know when you're not being completely honest. Not to mention, I've noticed you wince anytime Lachlan mentioned Gideon today. He may not have picked up on it. Or maybe he did and didn't want to say anything. But I'm your mother. I earned the right to call you out on your bullshit after enduring thirty hours of labor."

This was one of the main reasons I wanted to come out here. Not just to get away from California and everything going on, but so my mother could help me figure out which way was up. Sure, I could have talked to Melanie. But I needed someone who could look at the situation with fresh eyes. Who understood me the way only a mother could.

"You're right," I admitted with a deep exhale.

"I know." She gave me a playful wink as she took a sip of her champagne. Then she angled toward me, uncrossing and recrossing her legs.

She may not have noticed it, but I saw a few guys at

the other end of the bar checking her out. It didn't matter that she was in her fifties. My mom still looked amazing.

When I was her age, I hoped I looked as good in a little black dress as she did right now.

"So what's *really* going on?"

I stared into the distance, attempting to formulate my thoughts. But it all came down to one thing.

"I accused Gideon of being Samuel."

She sputtered around a mouthful of champagne. "You *what?*" she asked once she got her coughing fit under control. "I expected you'd tell me there was a little trouble in paradise. There always is in the beginning of a relationship. But to accuse him of being Samuel?" She shook her head in disbelief. "What triggered this?"

"Everything," I pushed out, relaxing into my chair as I replayed the last few weeks in my mind. "He's always reminded me of him. I understand he doesn't *look* like him, but he's always *felt* like Samuel," I said, not going into detail about *how* he felt like Samuel. "Then, when I went over to Liam's the other day, I overheard him talking with James about something the police found at Alton's cabin."

"What's that?" she prodded.

"A glass with Samuel's fingerprints on it."

She tilted her head, her brow furrowed. "I didn't read about that in any of the reports."

"I don't think they've released that information yet

since it's still an ongoing investigation. But hearing that…" I shook my head. "It unraveled me."

"I can imagine." She covered my hand with hers, giving it a squeeze.

"Melanie tried to talk some sense into me. At first, she did. Reminded me it's more probable that his prints were left on that glass from five years ago than for him to still be alive. But later that night, I couldn't sleep and ended up scrolling through old videos and photos of Samuel on my phone. And there was one of him playing with Ollie. He sounded so much like Gideon. Then I found a photo of Samuel without his shirt on and saw the scars on his torso, as well as the birthmark above his hipbone."

"And Gideon has those, too?"

I nodded. "Gideon has a *lot* of scars."

"From the car accident, right?"

"Yes. He also has burn marks in the same spot Samuel did."

"And the birthmark?"

I shrugged. "It *could* be the same, but there's a scar obscuring part of it."

She shifted her gaze forward, processing all of this before facing me once more. "And how did Gideon react?"

"He was definitely hurt. Accused me of only wanting to be with him because he reminds me of Samuel."

"Is that *why* you're with him?"

"No," I answered quickly, then sighed. "I don't know. From the beginning, there was something familiar about him. But is that why I was interested in him?" I shook my head. "I can't say. All I do know is that I feel like I'm losing my mind. One second, I'm convinced I'm crazy for even *thinking* he could be Samuel. The next, I can't help but think it's the only rational explanation for why Gideon would want to be with me. He's this ridiculously attractive, wealthy billionaire who could have anyone he wants. I'm a...a nobody."

An understanding smile grew on her lips as she placed a hand on my arm. "I know where you're coming from, Imogene. I've been exactly where you are now. Aside from accusing someone of being my ex. *That* would never happen." She snorted a small laugh, a hint of amusement dancing in her eyes before she schooled her expression, turning into the mom who always seemed to know what to say.

"When I met Lachlan, I constantly asked myself what he could see in me. Hell, when I realized who he was and that his sister was a true crime podcaster who had been looking into recent deaths she thought were inspired by—"

"I know," I interjected so she didn't have to say my sperm donor's name.

I probably could have counted on one hand the

number of times either of us had uttered it in the past decade.

"After learning that, I convinced myself that was why he was spending time with me. Not because he was interested in me, but because he hoped to get information."

"When did you know it was the real deal? That he wanted to be with you for you, not because of anything else?"

"When I admitted who I was, what I'd been through because of..." She trailed off, her eyes glossing over as she swallowed hard. "The raw agony I saw on your step-father's face, Imogene." She shook her head, taking a few moments to collect herself.

"In retrospect, I think I knew from the second he helped me after I was stung by a jellyfish, but the moment I allowed him to see the real me solidified it. That's the mark of real love. Not sending flowers or buying jewelry or romantic dinners. Acknowledging one's past and accepting it as if it's your own? There's no greater gift. Lachlan's done that from the beginning, even when I was too stubborn to admit it."

With a sideways glance, she studied my reaction to her words with intense scrutiny. "And something about the way I saw you interact with Gideon makes me think he's done that, too."

Memories of our short time together flooded back.

From the first time I noticed him during one of my morning runs, the way the heat of his stare sent a shiver down my spine. To the first time I spoke with him when I asked him to watch Gertie, my surfboard. To when I was nearly killed in that alley and he came to my rescue. To him showing up at the hospital with a change of clothes. To his surprise birthday gift of a dress I'd been fawning over, along with a day at the spa with Melanie. To our stolen moments during my birthday party when we couldn't keep our hands off each other. To finally allowing myself to open my heart again after losing Samuel.

To the moment Gideon opened himself to me, allowing me to see all his scars, both inside and out.

To the moment I allowed him to see all *my* scars, too, both inside and out.

To him accepting them as his, just as I did.

Maybe it *was* fate, like the barista at The Daily Grind stated. Maybe there wasn't anything nefarious about our meeting. Maybe he simply saw me and felt the same inexplicable pull I had.

"I'm not saying it's always going to be easy," Mom cut through, her voice tender and understanding. "Unfortunately, you grew up thinking you could trust a man who ended up betraying that trust in the worst way imaginable. It's only natural for you to always wait for the other shoe to drop, so to speak. I still struggle with it myself, even though Lachlan and I have been married for over a decade. The key is to find someone who understands your fears, your past, but still embraces them all the same. But you have to *let* him embrace them."

As I listened to her words, my lips lifted in the corners, my brain no longer clouded with any deceitful reason for why Gideon would want to be with me. Instead, all I could think about were the incredible things he'd done for me. Did he have his faults? Of course. But so did I.

"Based on that smile, I'm guessing Gideon's done that."

"He's repeatedly told me that my time with Samuel made me into the woman I am today. That he's falling for *that* woman. And what do I do?" I blew out a soft laugh, silently berating myself for my behavior. "Accuse him of being my dead boyfriend, all because Samuel's fingerprints, in all probability, were left on that glass when he was alive. Why can't I just enjoy this, instead of finding a reason to doubt him at every turn?" I asked rhetorically, but my mom didn't take it that way.

Or maybe she saw it as another opportunity to give me advice.

"Because that's what you're still hard-wired to do after living with a narcissistic sociopath for the first several years of your life." She placed her hand over mine once more, giving it a gentle squeeze. "Don't let him win.

Don't let him still have this control over you. You know what they say, don't you? About the best form of revenge?"

I nodded. "Living well."

"That's right. It's time for you to live well, Imogene. Regardless of whether that includes a certain tall, dark, and handsome man or not. But I have a feeling it does." She winked.

"Maybe," I replied mischievously.

"On that note..." She scooted off the barstool with effortless grace. "I need the ladies' room. Take it from me. Getting old sucks. I feel like I have to pee every twenty minutes, thanks to you."

"You love me," I sang.

She wrapped her arms around me, kissing my cheek. "More than anything." She gave me one last squeeze, then released me, making her way through the bar and toward the ladies' room.

As I continued to sip on my drink, my eyes went to my phone. I hadn't spoken to Gideon since our argument, but I needed to let him know I felt horrible. At least until I could tell him in person.

Grabbing my phone, I navigated to my most recent text exchange with Gideon and started typing.

ME:

I don't expect you to respond, and you don't have to. I know I fucked up, and I own that.

I still have a hard time wondering what someone like you could see in me, so I jump to ridiculous conclusions, like accusing you of being my boyfriend who's somehow managed to come back from the dead.

Which is impossible.

He's gone.

I know that.

Long story short, I still have trust issues.

I'm not making excuses. That's not the purpose of this message.

I just want you to know that I'm sorry.

I get that apologizing in a text is lame, but until I can do it face-to-face, if you even want to see me again after the way I treated you, this will have to do.

I'm sorry.

I'm still falling for you.

But I understand if you're no longer willing to fall with me.

As I hit send on my final text, I took another large

swallow of my drink, watching the status change from delivered to read.

I prayed I'd soon see the little dots appear below my message, indicating he was typing a response.

But I never did.

I couldn't blame him if he no longer wanted to pursue things with me. I'm not sure I'd be so quick to forgive if the shoe were on the other foot.

If I learned anything from this ordeal, it was that it was time to let Samuel go.

For once and for all.

Otherwise, I'd keep sabotaging my future. And Gideon *could* be my future. Or he could have been had I just thought rationally instead of jumping to insane conclusions.

Pushing out a long sigh, I returned my phone to my purse, more than aware I'd drive myself crazy looking at it all night if I didn't. My mother didn't see me much these days. She deserved my full attention.

I brought my glass back to my lips, hoping the alcohol would lessen the heartache, when a prickle of awareness trickled down my spine, followed by a hand grazing my shoulder blades.

I turned around, about to berate whoever thought he could touch me without my permission.

But any protest immediately left me when I was met with Gideon's familiar gaze.

CHAPTER THIRTEEN

Imogene

How was this possible? How was he here? I didn't tell him I was in Atlanta. I hadn't spoken to him since he stormed out of my townhouse in the early hours of yesterday morning. I must have been dreaming. Or I'd officially lost my mind.

Those were the only possible explanations for why Gideon Saint was currently standing in front of me, his body clad in a perfectly tailored designer suit that made him look as delicious as sin.

Just as deadly, too.

"Wha-what are you doing here?" I asked, snapping out of my shock.

"The same thing as you, it seems," he replied coolly.

"Having a drink with your mother?" I blurted out before I could stop myself.

His expression faltered. "I'm no longer afforded the opportunity, I'm afraid."

"Right." I winced, briefly squeezing my eyes shut. "I'm sorry. I didn't mean—"

"I'm in town on business," he interrupted, saving me from having to make yet another apology. "And if I'm being honest, I was stalking your social media profile when I noticed you post a photo of you and your mother in this very bar. Call me a hopeless romantic, but I couldn't help but think it was a sign. Or fate."

"Fate?" I repeated, reminded of the barista's words.

"Perhaps." He gestured toward my mom's vacant chair. "May I?"

I glanced past him and toward the hallway leading to the restrooms. My mom gave me an encouraging smile, along with an exaggerated wink before refocusing her attention on her phone.

One thing was certain. I had the coolest mom around. I didn't know many other women my age whose mothers would be their wingman.

Or wingwoman.

Returning my attention to Gideon, I nodded. "Sure."

"Thank you."

He unbuttoned his suit jacket and slid onto the barstool, his eyes focused forward, his expression pensive. The air between us crackled with the same intensity it always had. But tonight it felt even more powerful. Even more explosive.

Even more dangerous.

When I wasn't sure how much longer I could take the mounting tension, he finally spoke. "I'm sorry, too."

"What?" I furrowed my brow. "Why? You have nothing to apologize for, Gideon. I was—"

He grabbed my hands in his, the warmth of his touch seeping into my marrow.

"You've been through a lot over the past few days. Honestly, I don't know how I'd react if I learned the fingerprints of someone I cared for and who was supposed to be dead were recently found on a glass. I'd probably be clinging to hope just like you are, even though I know it's not possible."

"It's still no—"

"Do you remember what I told you?" he interrupted.

"You've told me a lot of things." I bit my bottom lip. "Some of which I'm not sure I can repeat in public."

He flashed me a conniving grin, the heat in his stare causing my core to clench, especially when he leaned closer, his gaze dipping to the cleavage of my dress.

"And I'll happily say all those things to you again." He lingered for a beat before pulling back, his expression turning serious once more. "I told you I didn't mind you bringing up your past or Samuel. That your past made you into the woman you are now."

He moved a hand to my cheek and gently cupped it.

"That still remains true, Imogene, despite my behavior. I *am* still falling for that woman. More every damn minute. If there's anyone who should apologize, it's me. I fucked up."

"So did I. Like I said in my text, I have trouble trusting people. I'm always looking for an ulterior motive for why someone would be interested in me."

"I'd be lying if I said my intentions have *always* been pure." His gaze roamed over me with a possessive hunger.

"Is that right?" I retorted in a husky voice, squeezing my thighs together to dull the throbbing need filling me from his proximity. His voice. His scent.

"I do quite enjoy making you come, Imogene," he whispered in a low, gravelly voice that made my entire body ache for his touch. "It gives me immense...pleasure. The way you move. The way you feel. There's nothing better."

When he inched toward me, my lips parted as the promise of his kiss hung in the space between us. But instead of giving me what I'd been craving since he left yesterday morning, he pulled back, leaving me a frustrated bundle of need.

"But that's not why I like spending time with you,"

he stated, taking my hand in his and brushing my knuckles. "I like spending time with you because you make me feel alive. I forgot what that was like," he mused absent-mindedly as he studied our joined hands. "So maybe we give this another shot," he suggested, his voice stronger once more. "And this time, I'll do everything in my power to make sure we don't get into another argument."

"I wouldn't go that far." I smirked, playfully waggling my brows.

"No?" He tilted his head.

"Because then we'd miss out on having makeup sex." I curved toward him. "And Gideon?"

"Yes?" His voice cracked.

There was something incredibly powerful about the idea that I was able to get under his skin. When I first met him, especially after witnessing him take out my attacker, I thought he was invincible. Infallible. A god living amongst mortals.

Instead, he was just like everyone else.

Just as *scarred* as everyone else.

His were just more visible than most.

"I *really* like makeup sex," I murmured, my breath kissing his lips.

Without a single care for the fact we were surrounded by dozens of people, Gideon gripped the back of my neck and slammed his mouth against mine, his tongue teasing and torturing. I whimpered, drowning in his kiss after too long without it.

"Goddamn, the sounds you make drive me crazy," he growled against my lips before taking them in another rough and desperate kiss, only to pull away moments later, leaving me panting and hungry for more.

"Check, please." His strong voice carried through the darkened space as he signaled the bartender, the power and dominance he exuded causing a shiver to roll through me.

"But my mom," I protested, suddenly remembering why I was here in the first place. "I can't ditch her."

As if on cue, my phone buzzed in my clutch. I retrieved it, laughing to myself when I read her text.

MOM:

I took an Uber home. Enjoy your evening with Gideon. I don't expect to see you home until tomorrow morning. That's an order.

"I may have the best mom ever. She's pretty much demanding I have sex with you." I turned my phone toward him.

"You really shouldn't disobey your mother. Otherwise, you might be punished."

"And we wouldn't want that." I leaned toward him and trailed a light finger down his chest, stopping just short of his crotch. "Would we?"

"Goddammit," he groaned, his jaw tense, nostrils flaring. "Where is the fucking check? You know what? Screw it."

He jumped to his feet and retrieved several large bills from his wallet, slamming them onto the counter. Then he hauled me off my stool and out of the bar, his strides long and determined as he pulled me down the sidewalk, his calloused hand clasped tightly around mine.

"Slow down," I gasped through my laughter as I struggled to keep up, especially in these heels.

But he didn't slow down. Instead, he stopped abruptly and took in my appearance, his ravenous eyes flaming as they roamed over my body, from the short blue dress to my ample cleavage, all the way down to my exposed legs.

Before I could react, he swept me into his arms and carried me as if I weighed nothing.

"What are you doing?" I squealed through even more laughter, my heart expanding when I heard a few women remark how they wished their significant other would do something as romantic as this.

"You were having trouble keeping up with me. So I'm carrying you. Problem solved."

"In a rush to get somewhere?" I flirted.

His blue eyes turned even darker as he narrowed them on me. "You have no idea."

CHAPTER FOURTEEN

Gideon

Imogene's laughter echoed around me as I rushed through the lobby, ignoring the whispers and upturned noses of the guests mingling in the luxurious space. Let them look. I didn't care what they thought about me. All I cared about was being with this woman.

But even as I basked in the melody of her infectious giggles, a voice that sounded suspiciously like Henry's taunted me from the recesses of my subconscious, reminding me this charade with Imogene would only become harder to maintain as time went on.

He was right.

Hell, that was why I used her accusation that I was Samuel as a reason to walk away. She was already dangerously close to unraveling everything.

I should have known I wouldn't be able to stay away for long. Not when Imogene had always been the one person to make me feel this way.

When I started down this road, I thought it would be easy to kill. During my years of captivity, I'd taken more lives than I cared to admit.

That was when I didn't have a choice.

It was either kill or be killed.

I killed to survive.

Now, I killed for revenge.

And each death hit me differently than I thought they would. Each life I took also took something from me.

A piece of my humanity.

After killing Brian McGuire, I needed to feel human again. Like less of the monster I was becoming every day.

Which was why I sought out Imogene tonight. She didn't need to know I'd been watching her for months now and knew the second she booked that flight to Atlanta.

All she needed to know was I believed it was fate I ended up coming out here for business. And that the only reason I knew she was at that bar was because she conveniently posted a photo to her social media account with the bar's logo visible behind her.

With every lie I told, I was just digging myself

deeper and deeper, but I needed just one more hit of Imogene. One more night of feeling human.

"Hurry up," I ground out as I jabbed at the door close button on the elevator, ready to throttle anyone who even thought about stepping inside. I was that desperate to lose myself in Imogene.

It had only been a little more than a day since I'd been alone with her, but it seemed like so much longer.

Then again, a lot had happened in that short time. A lot had changed.

I wasn't going to think about any of that right now, though. Not now that I had Imogene for however long I was able to keep her.

When the doors finally shut and the elevator began its slow ascent, I carefully set her down on her feet and our eyes locked. The small space crackled with electricity, my pulse increasing in time with Imogene's heaving chest.

As if able to read each other's minds, I moved toward her at the same time as she lunged for me, our bodies colliding in an erotic dance we were powerless to resist.

"Why did I think I could stay away?" I mused to myself.

"I don't know," Imogene panted as I peppered kisses from her mouth and along her jawline. "But it was fucking torture. I started to worry I'd have to actually unpack more of my boxes at my townhouse."

"Why's that?" I lifted my eyes toward hers, her skin already red from my rough kisses.

"So I could find my vibrator. You've spoiled me with all the orgasms you've given me lately."

"Well, then…" I gripped her hip, my mouth inching closer to hers with every breath. "I'll do my best to delay your need to unpack for as long as possible. But I must confess…"

"What's that?"

"I wouldn't mind using your vibrator on you. In fact, the idea turns me on quite a bit."

Smirking, she smoothed her hand down my shirt.

Unlike at the restaurant, she didn't stop when she reached my belt. She continued past it, brushing against my erection as she hoisted herself onto her toes, her lips skimming my neck.

"I can *feel* that."

Before I could force her mouth back to mine, the elevator jolted to a stop and the door slid open. With a seductive look, she lowered herself to her heels and turned, her hips swaying as she walked out of the elevator.

I barreled out after her, tugging her down the hallway toward my room. After fumbling for my keycard in my wallet, I held it up to the door. The second I heard it unlock, I flung it open, hauling her into my suite.

The door was barely closed before I crashed my lips against hers again, my hands roaming over her body as I guided her through the living room and into the bedroom. Kicking off her heels, she pushed my jacket down my shoulders, eagerly reaching for the buttons on my shirt.

Suddenly, she tore out of the kiss, bringing her fingers in front of her and examining them with a furrowed brow.

Panic raced through me at the sight of a few droplets of blood staining her skin. It wasn't much, but it didn't take much to condemn a man.

"What's this?" she asked, concern evident in her voice. "Did something happen? Are you hurt?" She scanned my frame, looking for any sign of injury, but she wouldn't find any.

After all, it wasn't my blood.

"Must have nicked myself shaving." I grabbed a tissue off the desk, wiping the blood off her fingers and shoving it into my pocket as I made a mental note to dispose of this suit first thing tomorrow morning.

I'd changed after finishing with Brian. I could only assume, in my desperate need to feel Imogene, I overlooked some blood elsewhere on my body.

What else did I overlook?

"Are you sure?" She raked her gaze over me.

"How else would I have gotten blood on my jacket?"

I remarked, the guilt festering in my stomach increasing by the second.

How many lies would I tell this woman? She didn't deserve this. But I needed her tonight. Needed the one person who always made it hurt less.

"Now where were we?" I pulled her closer, praying she didn't press the issue further. "I think you were about to take my shirt off."

She eyed me for another protracted beat before her mouth curved up into a smile, the blood now long forgotten.

At least by her.

"I was," she admitted in a sultry tone, her fingers trailing down my chest.

"Then what are you waiting for?"

She swiped her tongue along her lips, looking at me with hooded eyes, as if I was a delicious meal she was about to devour. God, I loved the heat in her stare when she got like this. When she was able to let go of the person she thought she needed to be and just be herself. I was so damn grateful she let me see this side of her.

"Just trying to savor the moment," she cooed, slowly unbuttoning my shirt. "Why rush things when we have all night?" Pushing the fabric down my arms, she ran her hands up my bare torso, her nails lightly raking into my skin.

I growled, wrapping my hand around her hair and

forcing her head back, giving me better access to her throat.

"Because you've already been driving me crazy all night, Imogene." I left rough kisses along her fair skin. "Do you have any idea how much I wanted to gouge out the eyes of everyone in that bar who so much as looked your way?"

"No one was looking at me."

"They were *all* looking at you." I cupped her breasts and squeezed her nipples through her dress, eliciting a yelp that turned into a pleasure-filled moan. "Imagining what it would be like to kiss you." I dipped toward her and covered her mouth with mine, my tongue tangling with hers. "What it would be like to touch you."

As I skimmed the curve of her frame, she writhed against me, especially when my hand slipped underneath the tiny skirt of her dress.

"What it would be like to fuck you." I pushed her soaked panties aside and pressed my thumb against her clit.

"Gideon," she whimpered, her legs shaking as I slipped a finger inside of her.

"This cunt is mine, Imogene."

"Yes," she exhaled.

"Say it," I growled, unsure why I needed to hear these words so much. It wouldn't change anything. Wouldn't change the lies I'd told her.

But I needed to know she was still mine, at least for tonight.

"I'm yours, Gideon. All of me." She clutched my face, forcing my eyes to hers. "You own all of me. My past." She touched a kiss to my cheek. "My present." She kissed the other cheek, then pulled back. "And my future."

I swallowed hard, my chest aching from the raw sincerity in her words. How did I repay her? By deceiving her. Betraying her.

Using her.

Instead of walking away before hurting her even more, I crushed my lips against hers in a desperate attempt to regain some semblance of control over something.

Anything.

I thrust my fingers even harder inside her, propelling her higher and higher with each fevered drive. When I felt her body tense around me, her orgasm imminent, I pulled my fingers from her, spinning her around to face the mirror on the wall opposite us. Her heavy pants filled the room, but she didn't question me.

Instead, she submitted to me completely, meeting my gaze in the mirror as I slowly lowered the zipper of her dress, sliding it down her frame along with her panties until she stood exposed before me.

She tried to face me, but I kept her locked in place,

smoothing my hand along her torso, committing every curve to memory, although I could already draw every inch of her with my eyes closed. The shape of her nipples. The fullness of her lips. Right down to the jagged line of the scar over her heart.

I reverently traced my fingers over it before taking a breast in my hand, my dick throbbing with the need to fuck her. But I needed this more. The buildup. The anticipation. The way her body squirmed in response to my touch. It was incredibly gratifying.

"Gideon, please," she begged as I rolled a nipple between my fingers.

"What do you need?"

"To feel you."

I gently rocked my hips against her. "You do feel me."

"That's not what I mean." Her voice dripped with desperation, her body throbbing with need. "It hurts, this ache inside me."

"Then let me make you feel good."

I abruptly spun her around, moving her to the edge of the bed and lowering her onto it. My knees hit the floor in front of her, and I spread her legs wide, admiring her glistening pussy. Without wasting another second, I plunged my tongue deep inside her, eliciting a loud moan as she fell back onto the mattress.

"No, Imogene. Watch."

She snapped her eyes open, propping herself onto her elbows to meet my hungry stare, her desire coating my lips and beard.

"I don't want you to take your eyes off that mirror. If you do, I won't let you come. I want you to see what I do when I make you come. Want you to see how goddamn beautiful you are when you let go. Want you to watch me own this cunt." I dragged a finger along her center, causing her to squirm. "Own you."

I kept my gaze trained on her as I circled her clit with my tongue. As instructed, she didn't fall back on the bed. Instead, her eyes remained locked on the mirror as she watched her reaction to my ministrations. Every so often, I noticed her close her eyes, so I retreated, denying her of the orgasm she was desperate for.

That was all it took for her to snap them open and watch herself again.

"Do you see how incredible you look?" I rasped out as I drove my fingers inside her. "How flushed your perfect skin gets when you're on the cusp of ecstasy?"

"Gideon, please. This is torture."

"You haven't seen torture, baby."

"I need to come so bad. Need you to make me come."

"Be a good girl and ask nicely."

"Please, Gideon. Please make me come."

"Gladly." I returned my mouth to her, my tongue

circling her clit as I hooked my fingers around to hit the spot that set her off.

"Oh, god," she mewled.

"Don't look away, Imogene," I reminded her gruffly. "Watch what I do to you. What only *I* do to you. Never forget it."

"Never again."

"Good." I dragged my tongue along her clit once more, this time adding my teeth as I sucked it into my mouth.

She detonated around me, her cries of pleasure echoing in the room as she came undone.

And like the good girl she was, she watched the entire thing through the mirror.

Her body was still convulsing when I stood up and flipped her onto her stomach.

"Hands and knees," I demanded as I toed out of my shoes, swiftly pushing down my pants and boxer briefs.

She eagerly obeyed my command, pulling herself up to her knees and resting on her forearms. When I kneeled behind her and brought my erection up to her, a moan slipped from my throat, the need to lose myself in her a strong compulsion I was too weak to resist.

"Gideon, please," she begged when I didn't immediately thrust into her. "I need to feel you. Need to feel whole again."

I squeezed my eyes shut. Her words alone should

have been enough for me to walk away. It was the right thing to do. The *honorable* thing to do.

But I wasn't an honorable man.

Not anymore. I stopped being honorable the second Liam Pierce pointed a gun at me and fired.

So instead, I drove inside of her with ruthless abandon, using her to chase away my demons.

Even if it was the last time I ever would.

CHAPTER FIFTEEN

Imogene

I blinked my eyes open and slowly roused myself from sleep, my body deliciously sore after last night's calisthenics.

When I agreed to go out for a few drinks with my mom, the last thing I expected was for Gideon to show up at the same bar. And I certainly never expected for him to apologize.

I thought I was the one in the wrong. Not him.

Still, he wouldn't let me shoulder the full blame for our falling out.

It was something Samuel always did, too.

But instead of resorting to my old ways, I pushed the notion aside. I almost lost Gideon because I was stuck in the past.

No more.

Now, I would only live in the present.

Like I should have done years ago.

I rolled over in bed, expecting to find Gideon sleeping beside me, but he wasn't there, the sheets cool. Instead, a folded piece of stationary was in his place.

I picked it up and smiled at his masculine hand-writing.

Which looked nothing like Samuel's.

Because he wasn't Samuel.

Imogene,

You looked so peaceful that I didn't want to wake you. I've taken the liberty of having some clothes delivered for you. They're in the top drawer of the dresser. Of course, if you'd prefer to stay naked, you won't hear any complaints from me.

Yours,

G

It was probably nothing for a man with his resources, but it meant a lot that he made sure I had daytime attire so I didn't have to do the walk of shame in such a luxurious hotel while wearing my dress from last night. This was just the type of person Gideon Saint was. He may have tried to convince me he wasn't a good person on countless occasions, but I saw past his tough exterior to the compassionate man hidden beneath the layers of scars. I would never take that man for granted again.

Climbing out of bed, I headed toward the dresser and opened the top drawer, finding yoga pants, jeans, some fresh underwear, as well as a few t-shirts, all the correct size and the same style I typically wore.

As thoughtful as the gesture was, I had another idea.

Biting my lower lip to reel in my smile, I opened the closet door and examined Gideon's crisp suits, opting for one of his oversized dress shirts instead. I fastened only a few of the bottom buttons, leaving quite a bit of my cleavage exposed. Then I slipped out of the bedroom and into the living room.

Gideon sat at the dining room table and sipped on a coffee, a feast spread out before him — eggs benedict, fresh fruit, a stack of pancakes dripping with syrup, even bagels and smoked salmon. I couldn't help but admire him as his gaze skimmed the pages of a newspaper.

It reminded me of what the barista said the other morning. How he was one of the few people who wasn't constantly glued to his cell phone.

Until we exchanged numbers, I'd never even seen him look at a cell phone. Instead, whenever we were together, I had his full attention, a rarity these days. Even

I was guilty of mindlessly scrolling through my phone. Not Gideon, though.

Sensing my presence, he looked up from the newspaper and paused mid-sip, his eyes flaming as he drank me in.

"Goddamn," he hissed, folding his newspaper and returning his coffee to the table as I sauntered toward him.

With a seductive smile, I hoisted myself onto the surface mere inches in front of him. Plucking a strawberry off one of the many plates covering the table, I brought it up to my lips and took a slow, tantalizing bite. Gideon's jaw clenched, his nostrils flaring as his gaze zeroed in on my mouth.

"What's for breakfast?" I asked nonchalantly, as if it were completely normal for me to sit on the dining room table, dressed only in one of his suit shirts, my breasts barely covered.

"I believe my appetite has changed since placing my room service order," he said in a low voice.

"Is that right?"

As I uncrossed and recrossed my legs, his pupils flamed, his stare dipping to my waist.

"Most definitely." He slid his hands up my thighs, his touch rough yet gentle at the same time.

Just as he was about to reach my center, a chiming cut through. Cursing under his breath, he reached into the inside pocket of his suit jacket and pulled out his phone.

"I fucking hate these things," he growled.

"Something wrong?" I purred.

"Yes," he replied through gritted teeth. "I have a beautiful woman wearing only my shirt sitting on the table with what I can only assume to be a dripping wet pussy begging to be devoured, and this thing has the audacity to remind me of a meeting I have this morning."

"A meeting?" I tilted my head as he typed feverishly on his phone.

"Sadly, this isn't strictly a trip for pleasure." He clicked off his phone and returned it to his jacket, his attention fully devoted to me once more. "Although I enjoyed quite a bit of pleasure last night." He waggled his brows.

"Is that right?" I cooed, slowly unbuttoning my shirt.

His shirt.

"That's right." He swallowed hard, his breathing increasing with every inch of skin I exposed to him.

It didn't matter that we spent all night tangled up in each other without a single scrap of fabric between us. He still admired me as if this were the first time he ever saw me.

As if I were the most beautiful woman in the world.

"Well, if you have important business to attend to, I

don't want to interfere." I smirked as I slid his shirt off my shoulders.

I shouldn't have felt as empowered as I did, considering I was completely naked while he was fully dressed. But the way his hungry gaze drank me in made me feel desired and wanted.

"You know what they say, don't you?"

"What's that?" I chewed on my bottom lip.

"Breakfast is the most important meal of the day."

With a firm touch, he pressed a hand to my shoulder, forcing me to lie on my back. Moving his chair closer, he spread my legs as wide as they would go.

"And I really shouldn't start my morning without a balanced breakfast," he rasped before burying his face between my thighs and devouring me like it was his last meal.

"Do you think I can steal you again tonight?" Gideon asked as he walked me to the door after I showered and dressed. "I have some prior commitments throughout the day, but I should be free by seven or eight. I don't want to take you away from your parents," he added quickly. "I can't seem to get enough of you." He dipped his head toward me, his lips feathering against mine in an achingly tender kiss.

How could I say no when he kissed me like this? So soft and sweet.

"My mom will understand. Hell, based on last night, she may *demand* I spend the night with you again."

"Then it's a date. I'll pick you up once I'm free."

"Or I can meet you here. That way, when you get back after a long day of...whatever it is you do, I'll be waiting for you in the bar." Grinning mischievously, I lifted myself onto my toes, my breath kissing his neck. "I'll be the one in a short dress and no panties."

A low groan fell from his throat and his grip on my hip tightened. "Knowing that will make it impossible for me to think about anything else."

"Then you'd better hurry home to me," I teased as I touched my lips to his in a ghost of a kiss.

Then I spun on my heels and slipped into the hallway. When I felt the tiny hairs all over my body stand on end, I glanced behind me to find Gideon watching my every move.

And the look he gave me was pure sin and danger wrapped together in an intoxicating combination.

"Tonight," he said, the word a cross between a promise and a threat.

"Tonight," I repeated before continuing toward the elevator.

When the doors opened, I stood back to allow

another guest to step out. But *who* that guest was froze me in my tracks.

It was like being sent back in time.

Which was the last thing I needed, considering I just vowed to stop thinking about the past.

To stop thinking about Samuel.

But that was easier said than done when Henry Fontaine, Samuel's foster brother and best friend, currently slid past me, his attention focused on his cell phone as he feverishly typed at it.

"Henry?" I called out.

The instant he heard my voice, he came to an abrupt stop, darting his head up.

As his green eyes locked with mine, they widened with a mixture of confusion and panic before his expression softened, as if snapping out of whatever stupor he was in.

"Imogene." He dropped his phone into the pocket of his jeans and wrapped me in a hug, kissing my cheek. "How are you?"

"Good. Really good, actually." I tried to hide my blush, considering the reason I was doing so good was because Gideon just fucked me so hard I saw stars.

"I'm glad to hear that." He released me, stepping back. "What are you doing here?"

"Just visiting a friend. I came home for the weekend

to see my parents and he's staying here," I rambled nervously, not sure I should have been talking to Samuel's best friend about my current dating life. "Are you still in cyber security?" I asked in an effort to change the subject.

"More or less."

"Still have an office downtown?"

He nodded. "As well as locations in Boston, New York, Chicago, and LA."

"No shit? I just moved to San Diego. And Melanie lives in Santa Monica. Next time I visit her, I'd love to get together if you're in the area."

"I'll let you know," he responded, running his fingers through his dark hair. "I never know where I'll be one day to the next. Some of my clients can be demanding." He flashed me a smile.

Despite the fact that he was a couple of years older than Samuel, he still had a boyish appearance, making him look no older than thirty. Especially when he smiled and his dimples popped.

It didn't help matters that, despite his success these past few years, he still dressed in faded jeans and vintage band t-shirts. Then again, so did Samuel, refusing to wear suits, even during investor meetings, which annoyed Liam to no end.

Yet another reason I was crazy to think Gideon was Samuel.

It was rare to see Gideon in anything other than a suit.

Samuel avoided wearing suits at all costs.

"I hate to cut this short, but I need to get going," he said, anxiously shifting from foot to foot.

"Right. Of course. It was good seeing you."

"You, too." He left me with another hug before continuing down the hallway.

In the direction of Gideon's suite.

I told myself it didn't mean anything. It was merely a coincidence I ran into Henry in this hotel, on this floor. He was probably here to see a client. Or maybe a woman.

But just before getting on the elevator, I stole one last glance down the hallway, if for no other reason than to erase any remaining suspicion.

In my life, there have been many moments I wish I could get a do-over. Could go back to and choose a different path. Go down a different road.

This was one of those moments.

Because when I peeked around the corner and saw Henry pull out a keycard and let himself into Gideon's suite, there were now just *too* many coincidences for me to ignore.

CHAPTER SIXTEEN

Gideon

"What the fuck are you doing?" Henry seethed the second he walked into my suite.

I snapped my head away from my laptop, where I'd been watching the security feed from the funeral home now that I was alone.

Based on what I'd been able to decipher so far, none of Brian McGuire's employees suspected any foul play. All they knew was he hadn't shown up for work, leaving the assistant funeral director to take charge of a viewing scheduled for this afternoon.

"What are you talking about?"

He stormed toward me. "I just ran into Imogene as I was getting off the goddamn elevator. On this fucking floor." He threw his hands up, exasperated. "You said you ended things."

"I did, but she apologized, and I figured I'd be a shit boyfriend if I didn't forgive her," I joked, hoping to lighten the mood.

But Henry was in no mood to joke this morning.

"You're not her boyfriend!" he bellowed, his voice shaking the crystal chandelier hanging over the dining room table. "You're lying to her. She's already questioning things. The more time you spend with her, the more *lies* you tell her, the riskier it gets. If you're going to carry on with whatever the fuck this is, she deserves to know the truth. *Now*. Or I'll do it for you."

"You wouldn't," I snarled.

He narrowed his venomous gaze at me. "If that's what it takes for you to finally get your head out of your goddamn ass, I will."

We glowered at each other for several long moments, neither one of us willing to back down just yet.

I was more than aware that last night shouldn't have happened. That I should have kept my distance from Imogene. And I certainly shouldn't have made plans to see her again tonight. But she was a damn drug.

Last night, she gave me exactly what I needed. Gave me back a piece of my humanity. It was selfish of me, but I wanted more of that. *Needed* more of that, especially with everything I had planned over the coming weeks.

But telling her the truth?

"She can*not* know," I declared vehemently.

"Why? What is so bad about finally telling her the truth? After everything she's been through, after everything *you've* put her through, don't you think she deserves that? Don't you think—"

"*Because I don't want her to know what I've become!*" I roared as I jumped to my feet, my biggest fear spilling from me before I could stop it.

I didn't think I'd ever tell anyone, including Henry.

But now it was out there. The real reason I couldn't stomach the idea of revealing myself to Imogene. It wasn't because I was worried she'd tell Liam or go to the police.

It was because I didn't want to do anything that would taint her memories of Samuel. Telling her the truth would do exactly that.

"You didn't hear how she talked about Samuel at the golf tournament." I rubbed my hand over my face, slinking into the leather chair. "She still loves him."

"*You,*" Henry responded firmly. "She still. Loves. You. Not this made up persona of Gideon Saint. But you. Samuel Tate. That's who you really are."

"No, Henry. I'm not. I may have the same DNA. But I haven't been Samuel Tate since that bastard pointed a gun at me and fired. I'd rather—"

A choked sob reverberated from the hallway, cutting

me off. It was muted, but in my mind it was as jarring as hearing a gunshot on a peaceful day, shattering everything in sight.

I darted my eyes toward the door, a sinking feeling forming in the pit of my stomach about what caused that noise.

Who caused that noise.

Slowly standing, I strode the few feet toward the door, my hand hovering over the knob with hesitation and dread.

Drawing in a shaky breath, I finally opened the door, not surprised to find Imogene mere feet away.

I thought the worst thing I'd ever seen was the look on her face when she learned Samuel's fingerprints had been found on a glass at Alton's cabin.

That was nothing compared to this.

The pain. The heartache. The betrayal.

It broke me.

There was no doubt she'd overheard every syllable I just said.

And every syllable Henry had said, too.

I instinctively stepped toward her, unsure what else to do. What to say to make it hurt any less.

"Don't touch me," she demanded, recoiling from me as if I were the devil incarnate.

In a way, I was.

At least I was *her* devil.

"Who..." Her voice caught in her throat as she struggled to get the words out. "Who are you?"

"You've known all along, Imogene," I responded calmer than I thought possible with all the emotions warring inside me. Anger. Frustration. Despair. They were all there, fighting for dominance.

"Your name," she ordered firmly, her voice no longer trembling. "Tell. Me. Your. Name."

"My legal name is Gideon Saint."

"Your *birth* name. What was your name when you were born?"

I squeezed my eyes shut as I pushed out a resigned breath. I hated everything about this. But Henry warned me this was a strong possibility. Or, more accurately, an inevitability. I just didn't think it would happen today. Thought I'd have a little more time. Thought I could have one more night with her.

I truly was a selfish bastard.

Finally, I shifted my gaze back toward hers. "Samuel Tate."

The instant my given name left my mouth, every muscle in her body gave out and she collapsed against the wall.

I moved to help her, but she vehemently shook her head, holding her arm defensively in front of her.

"Why?" she gasped, her breaths coming in ragged spurts.

I opened and shut my mouth several times, trying to figure out what to tell her.

It was one thing for her to know who I was.

It was another to tell her exactly why I'd been lying to her.

Instead, I turned back toward my suite, where Henry stood in the doorway, watching us with a mixture of pity and sorrow.

"Can you make sure she gets home okay?" I asked softly.

"I told—"

I cut him off with a sharp gesture of my hand. "I don't want to hear it right now. Just make sure she's okay."

"I don't think she'll ever be okay after this," he responded under his breath.

I chanced one last glimpse at Imogene, her expression pale.

As if she'd seen a ghost.

"Then make sure she's safe," I pleaded, my voice catching.

He gave me a solemn nod and moved toward Imogene, wrapping an arm around her waist, supporting her as he led her toward the elevators.

Once they disappeared from view, I stormed back into my suite, clenching and unclenching my fists as I paced the length of the bedroom.

No matter how hard I tried, I couldn't erase the sight of Imogene's anguished expression when I finally admitted the truth. It would remain one of my core memories until the day I died. Not the day I met my mentor. Or the day I graduated college. Or the day I learned my gaming platform had become an overnight success.

From this day forward, I would always remember the pain I caused Imogene Prescott because of my lies.

I collapsed onto the bed and buried my head in my hands, sucking in deep breath after deep breath, feeling like the world was falling apart around me. When I caught my reflection in the mirror, I could no longer recognize the man staring back.

Not because I'd changed my appearance. It was so much more than that. I couldn't stand looking at this face anymore. The face I was forced to wear after my old one was too beaten and damaged from years of abuse, leaving behind nothing but a shell of who I used to be.

All because the men I trusted betrayed me.

With a guttural roar, I leapt to my feet and slammed my fists into the mirror over and over again until nothing remained but my blood and hundreds of shards of glass, each one mocking me with everything that had been taken from me.

CHAPTER SEVENTEEN

Imogene

I didn't know how I got out of the hotel. Everything was a blur.

Everything except the truth that Gideon Saint *was* Samuel Tate.

Just like I suspected.

Everyone told me I was crazy.

Gideon told me I was crazy.

But I wasn't.

And now I was supposed to just accept the fact that the man I loved with every fiber of my being had been alive all these years? That he'd been lying to me?

I had so many questions. But one had been at the forefront of my mind the entire time I sat in the back seat of the SUV as Henry navigated the familiar streets of Atlanta.

"How?" I asked softly, my voice not sounding like my own.

"What's that?" Henry looked in the rearview mirror, briefly meeting my eyes.

"How is he still alive?" I said, this time more firmly.

Henry blew out a heavy sigh, his shoulders falling. "It's not my story to tell, I'm afraid."

"You have to give me something here because I don't know what to fucking think right now, Henry. I just…" I turned my gaze out the window, struggling to reel in my emotions.

I was trying so damn hard not to cry, but I didn't know how much longer I could keep it all in. Didn't know how much longer I could hold in the scream that was desperate to break free to drown out the agony taking root deep in my marrow.

"The first day I saw him, his eyes reminded me of Samuel's," I told him. "Then when I saw him up close, there was something so damn familiar about him. Not his appearance, but everything else. And when he told Ollie to heel?" I sucked in my quivering lip. "The only thing that made me think it couldn't be him was because he looks nothing like the Samuel I knew. *My* Samuel. His nose is too crooked. His cheekbones are too high. His jaw is too square and wide. What happened to him? How could he look so different?"

"Again, it's—"

"Not your story to tell," I snapped bitterly. "Got it." I exhaled a quivering breath as I crossed my arms over my stomach to fight off the chill overtaking me despite the sunshine streaming into the car through the windows. "What *can* you tell me?"

"I can tell you *my* story."

"And what's that?"

"I had a similar reaction when he showed up on my doorstep."

"When?" I furrowed my brow. "How long have you known?"

He hesitated before confessing, "a year."

"A year? You've known for a year and never..." I pushed down the betrayal bubbling inside me, unsure how much more I could take. "Why did he lie to me? Or is that not your story to tell, either?"

He briefly met my gaze through the mirror once more. "I'm sorry."

"But he was shot. They said he was dead," I choked out, tears stinging my eyes as I thought about all the pain and grief I'd endured. "I mourned him, Henry. Every fucking day. I *still* mourn him. And now?"

I dug my fingers through my hair, feeling like my brain was about to explode. "I'm just supposed to accept he's still alive? Why didn't he tell me? Why did he make me think I was losing my goddamn mind? Hell, he made *me* feel like a horrible person for asking if he was Samuel the other night. Accused me of living in the past. Of only wanting to be with him because he reminded me of Samuel, when the entire time…"

I swallowed hard through the ache in my throat. In my chest. In my soul.

"Why would he do this to me?" I squeaked out.

"He has his reasons."

"What could possibly be so important he'd go through all of this? And his face? Why did he change his appearance?"

"He didn't have a choice. I barely recognized him when he showed up at my front door. His face was so… disfigured. It wasn't until he told me a story from foster care no one else would know about that I knew it was him. He endured a lot in the time he was gone, Imogene."

He floated his gaze toward the mirror, allowing the truth of his statement to sink in, even if he couldn't share exactly *what* he'd been through.

"I'm not saying what he's done to you is right, and I cautioned him against this, but he's insisted it's worth the risk."

"What is?"

"Revenge."

The word hung heavy in the car as I attempted to wrap my head around everything.

If Henry thought it would give me answers, he was mistaken. Instead, it only brought forward more questions.

Questions I feared I'd never learn the answer to.

"Revenge against who? Me?"

He shook his head. "The people who did this to him. Who killed Sam. He truly believes that, while Sam's DNA may run through him, the Samuel Tate we both know and love *did* die in that car. Hell, for a while *I* believed that, too. Until..." He trailed off.

"Yes?"

He adjusted his grip on the steering wheel, turning down the street leading toward Chastain Park.

"Since he's been spending time with you, I've seen more and more of the man he used to be. The old Sam. He's still in there, even if he's buried underneath years of painful memories and trauma."

"What happened?" I asked again, partly to myself. Partly to see if Henry would actually respond this time.

"Like I said, it's not my story to tell."

"Will *he* ever tell me?"

"I hope so."

He steered the car up the long driveway leading to my parents' house, then put it in park, jumping out to open my door for me.

"I can manage on my own."

"I promised I'd make sure you made it home safely. That means into the house."

"Fine," I huffed, too exhausted to fight. Instead, I walked beside Henry toward the front door.

This was a path I'd walked hundreds of times in my life, but today it felt different. My brain rewound to the first time I brought Samuel home to meet my mom and Lachlan. He'd been so nervous about making a good first impression. Not just because he'd always been a huge fan of Lachlan's, but because of the nine-year age difference between us.

But my mom and Lachlan were the last people to judge a couple based on a difference in age. After all, Lachlan was thirteen years younger than my mom. Like she told me that night after Samuel left. Age was just a number. All that mattered was that he treated me right.

I told her he did.

What was I supposed to tell her now? How was I supposed to reconcile everything I now knew about Gideon Saint with the Samuel Tate who stole my heart?

I faced Henry as we reached the door. "Does he just expect me to hide his secret from everyone?"

"Knowing him like I do, I can all but guarantee he'd want you to do what you think is right."

"What *is* right?"

"You need to make that decision for yourself." He

pulled out his wallet and handed me a card. "If you need anything, call me. I mean it, Imogene." He gave me a concerned look. "If you notice anything out of the ordinary or suspicious, contact me immediately. No matter the time of day."

His words only added to my growing anxiety. "Why? What's going on, Henry? What aren't you telling me?"

"Just...promise me."

I glowered at him for several protracted moments, willing him to embellish further. But he remained as stoic as ever.

"Fine," I finally conceded. "I'll call you if anything comes up."

"Thank you."

He stepped back, but didn't immediately retreat, remaining true to his promise to see I made it home safely.

It wasn't until I punched my code into the door and slipped inside that he finally made his way back toward the driveway. Once he did, I released a long breath and leaned against the entryway wall, my mind reeling from how much of a turn this morning took.

All because I didn't get in that elevator when I should have.

A part of me wished I had.

But I had a feeling the truth would have come out

eventually, regardless of Gideon's constant manipulation.

It was ironic now that I thought about everything.

I fought with Liam because he was suspicious of Gideon. Convinced myself all of Liam's outrageous claims were just because he was trying to manipulate me again. All along, the only person manipulating me was Gideon.

"Imogene, sweetie. Is that you?" Mom called out from the kitchen, pulling me out of my mounting confusion.

I took another deep inhale, doing my best to remain strong. To act as if my entire world hadn't just been flipped upside down. Then I pushed off the wall and made my way toward the kitchen, plastering a smile on my face as I walked into my mom's outstretched arms.

"Hey, Mom."

"How was your night?"

"Good." It wasn't a total lie. My night *was* good. Mind blowing.

It was this morning that was anything but.

She pulled out of the hug, holding me at arm's length. "So you patched things up with Gideon, then?"

"It would appear so."

She looped an arm through mine, dragging me toward the island. "Did you know he'd be in town, or did he come all this way just to make things right?"

I parted my lips, but I was no longer sure of the truth. He claimed he was here on business and it was just a coincidence I was also here. Now I couldn't help but wonder if that was the truth or if he'd followed me out here.

It was yet another question to add to my list.

"I was certainly surprised to see him," I answered, hoping she'd leave it at that.

I should have known better.

"So tell me." She hoisted herself onto one of the barstools, patting the one beside it for me. "What did he say? What did *you* say?"

"I... I'm just really tired," I said, a wave of exhaustion washing over me from having to keep up the façade. "I'm going to lie down for a few hours, if you don't mind."

She straightened, studying me with a furrowed brow. "Sure. Of course."

"Thanks." I gave her a half-hearted smile, then started out of the kitchen.

"Are you sure everything's okay?" she called after me, and I paused in my tracks.

How was I supposed to answer that? Nothing was okay.

I wasn't sure anything ever would be again.

"Just...tired."

"Okay," she drew out.

But I could feel her skepticism from across the room.

After everything we endured together, she could pick up on my moods. Knew when I wasn't being completely honest.

What could I tell her, though?

No, Mom. I'm not okay. Not after learning that Gideon really is Samuel. That he never died. That he's been alive all this time, enduring god knows what, and now is out for revenge against the people who hurt him, whoever they may be.

Just the idea of admitting that twisted me up, causing the hurt from all the lies to fester even more, threatening to destroy me from the inside out.

As I entered my bedroom, I headed straight toward my ensuite bathroom, shedding the clothes Gideon bought for me. Or was it Samuel? I didn't even know what to call him. Didn't know who he was, despite what Henry told me.

Even though I'd recently showered, I turned on the water as hot as it would go and stepped under the scalding stream, hoping it would wash everything away.

But I doubted anything was that powerful.

CHAPTER EIGHTEEN

Gideon

The click of the door opening reached me in the bathroom, and I finished taping up my hands before rushing into the living room.

"How is she?" I demanded the instant I saw Henry.

"What the fuck happened to you?" His eyes zeroed in on my bandaged hands.

"Got into a little accident with the mirror." I waved him off, downplaying my injuries.

These wounds were nothing compared to some of the shit I'd suffered for years. Once I washed away the blood and shards of glass, it became clear that most of the cuts were superficial. In a few days, they would be nothing but faint scars.

Unfortunately, I couldn't say the same for the mirror.

Henry slipped past me and into the bedroom, taking in the mess I'd made. "A little accident?"

"I'll pay for a goddamn replacement. Just tell me how she is," I repeated, hoping he wouldn't press me about *why* I'd obliterated the mirror.

That I couldn't stand the sight of my face.

That I wasn't sure if I ever could again.

Not when it was yet another reminder of everything those bastards had taken from me.

"She's hurt," he finally answered as he returned to the living room and sank into the couch. "And really fucking confused, man."

"What did she say?" I sat beside him.

"She just wanted to know how this could be possible. What happened to you— or, Samuel," he corrected.

"What did you tell her?"

"That it's not my story to tell."

"And she was okay with that?"

He barked out a laugh. "I wouldn't say she was okay with it. She's not okay with any of this. I'm not sure I am, either." He leveled me with a glare, his disagreement with the path I'd chosen obvious. "But she understands the truth needs to come from you," he added before I could remind him of the promise he made when I'd first shared my plans with him.

I gave him the choice to walk away. Told him he

didn't have to be involved. But after uncovering what those bastards did to Jonah, he wanted revenge as much as I did. Vowed to do whatever was necessary to make sure they could never hurt another person.

"You lived it. Not me." His analytical gaze swept over my features. "You *are* going to tell her, aren't you?"

Shifting my eyes from his, I stood and strode toward the large windows overlooking Buckhead, the bustling streets of Atlanta moving thirty stories below.

"She knows who I am. What more is there?"

"A lot fucking more," he replied sharply, shooting to his feet. "Like the truth about what happened to you. Where you were for four goddamn years."

"I just want to keep her safe, Henry. The less she knows—"

"That argument might have worked before. It doesn't anymore. She knows who you are. That makes her a liability."

I spun around, eyes wide in panic, my pulse increasing. "A liability? What are you—"

"Not to you," he quickly assured me. "But to Liam. And James. Imagine how Liam would react if Imogene just so happens to say, 'Hey. Did you know Gideon Saint is actually Samuel Tate? Small world, right?'"

I blinked, my mind spinning with dozens of scenarios now that Imogene knew the truth.

At least enough of the truth to make it dangerous.

I hadn't considered it until now, too consumed with the raw agony I saw in Imogene's expression this morning. But Henry had a point. If she said something to Liam, it could have disastrous consequences. Not for me, but for her. Hell, Liam had hired someone to kidnap Imogene. There was no telling what he would do if she mentioned I was still alive. Only knowing bits and pieces was more dangerous for her than knowing everything.

"You just said all you care about is keeping her safe," Henry continued. "By *not* telling her, you're putting her life even more at risk. The only way to protect her is if she knows everything or nothing. Since nothing is no longer an option..."

I squeezed my eyes shut as I pinched the bridge of my nose, trying to come up with a single scenario where her knowing who I was wouldn't be a problem.

Liam had repeatedly demonstrated how far he was willing to go in order to control and manipulate Imogene. He was the most dangerous type of man. He'd make you think he was your best friend one minute, then stab you in the back the next.

Or, more appropriately, shoot you in the stomach.

If Imogene were to mention something to Liam, I had no doubt he'd silence her by whatever means necessary. He was already on edge with the body found on his boat, as well as the discovery of my fingerprints at Alton's cabin.

Things would only get worse once word about a missing funeral director finally started hitting the airwaves.

The same funeral director who was hired to clean up his mess.

"There's a risk she'll go to the police before I've finished," I said. "She could not only implicate me, but also you."

"I told you from the beginning." He placed his hand on my shoulder and squeezed. "I'm with you, no matter where this leads. Even if it's straight down to hell. I've got your back, brother. Always." He paused, his eyes locking on mine. "You have to decide what's more important to you. Imogene's safety. Or this vendetta."

I pulled away and ran my hand over my face as I exhaled a long breath, the weight of everything a suffocating weight on my chest.

Weeks ago, it wouldn't have even been a question. I lived and breathed revenge. I was a servant to my vengeance.

But now that I'd seen her tears as she continued to mourn the man I once was, I found myself feeling things I didn't think possible again.

I meant what I told her the other night. I *was* falling for her. And not as Samuel.

But as the man I was now.

There was a chance Imogene would turn me in once

she learned the extent of my depravity. But it was better than any harm coming to her. I'd never be able to live with myself if that happened.

Facing Henry, I gave him a subtle nod. "I'll tell her."

CHAPTER NINETEEN

Imogene

"Are you feeling more rested?" Mom asked later that afternoon when I finally emerged from my room and into the kitchen.

If it were up to me, I would have stayed in my bed all day, curled up in a ball as I attempted to make sense out of everything I learned. But that would only make her more suspicious. Would only cause her to ask questions I wasn't ready to answer.

I doubted I'd ever be.

"A little," I lied.

In reality, I hadn't slept a wink. How could I? My mind was consumed with thoughts and questions about Samuel and why he kept the truth from me.

"I'm about to whip up some of my strawberry shortcake cookies." She opened the cupboard door, pulling out the items she needed. "Want to help?"

"Actually, I'm thinking about going for a hike up Stone Mountain."

She dropped the armful of ingredients onto the island, her eyes narrowing on me. "Are you sure you're okay? Just yesterday, you told me how horrible you felt for accusing Gideon of being Sam. And now, after spending the night with him, you want to hike to one of your and Sam's favorite spots?"

If anyone would put two and two together, it was my mom. But I needed some fresh air. Needed to go somewhere with no distractions. Somewhere quiet. Peaceful. Where I could sort through my thoughts and feelings.

"I can't pretend he never existed."

"No one is asking you to." Approaching me, she ran her hands down my arms. "Just don't let this stand in the way of what you might have with Gideon. I did the same thing with Lachlan and almost lost him. Well, not the *same* thing, but I kept letting the past control me. I don't want you to make the same mistake."

Twenty-four hours ago, I would have promised I wouldn't.

That was before I learned my past *was* my present.

"I won't be long. Can I borrow your car?"

"Of course."

"Thanks."

I headed toward the refrigerator and filled up my water bottle. After grabbing a few protein bars from the cupboard and throwing them in my bag, I kissed my mom's cheek, then slipped out of the house and into her silver SUV, making the thirty-minute trek out of the city.

Despite having often hiked the trail up Stone Mountain with Samuel, being out here allowed me to think. No electronics. No distractions. Just me and nature. Plus, the view from the top couldn't be beat. While I preferred it around sunrise or sunset, it was still beautiful, especially on a clear day like today, the Atlanta skyline sprawled out in the distance.

Once I reached the top of the summit after the relatively easy mile-long hike, I sat close to the ledge and sipped on my water.

I hadn't been up here in years.

Not since my birthday five years ago.

This was where the last clue of the scavenger hunt Samuel organized for me led.

A bittersweet smile tipped on my lips as memories of exploring the city through Samuel's carefully planned clues flooded back. Some of them were more challenging than others, but this one didn't require even a moment's thought on my part. I knew where to go the second I read it.

Where love happened.

This was the exact spot where Samuel told me he loved me for the first time.

And five years ago, this was where he told me he wanted to spend the rest of his life with me. That he was ready to tell Liam the truth.

How did I react? By panicking. Telling him I needed more time.

For years, I'd regretted the way I responded. Wished I'd told him I was ready. That I wanted him and only him.

After investigators found his car and he was presumed dead, I would have given anything to have another chance with him. For him to still be alive.

Well, I got my wish.

I just didn't expect it to be like this, tainted with lies and manipulation.

"This will always be my favorite view in the city," a familiar voice mused, cutting through my memories.

I jumped to my feet, sucking in a sharp breath when I saw Gideon standing mere inches away.

Or was he Samuel?

Right now, wearing a white t-shirt, gray shorts, and sneakers, he looked more like Samuel. He was even wearing a hat.

It was a stark contrast to the sophisticated man who I let have me for breakfast this morning.

"What are you doing here?" I demanded, pushing

down the bile rising in my throat from the reminder of his deception. His betrayal. Then I noticed the bandages wrapped around his hands. "What happened?"

"Got into a fight with a mirror," he replied with a hint of humor. "If you think this is bad, you should see the other guy."

Samuel would have said something like this. He always had an amazing ability to make light of stressful situations. It was one of the things I loved about him.

But I wasn't sure how to reconcile *that* Samuel with the man standing in front of me.

"How did you know I'd be here? Are you having me followed?" I crossed my arms in front of my stomach.

"I don't need to have you followed to know you'd want to come here. I know *you*, Imogene. That's enough."

"That makes one of us," I scoffed. "I have no idea who the hell you are. How you could have lied to me like this."

"Which is why I'm here."

"I don't know how you expected—" I stopped short when his words finally registered, my mouth snapping closed. "It is?" I furrowed my brows.

"Yes." He stepped toward me.

Unlike this morning, I didn't back up. Instead, I allowed myself to get lost in his eyes.

Samuel's eyes.

They seemed familiar the first time I saw them in the morning light. There was something about the atmosphere that day as I ran along the beach. Almost like I could feel his presence.

Truthfully, I'd felt as if Samuel were watching over me for a while now.

I guess he was.

"Was any of it real?" I choked out, my question leaving me before I could stop it.

"What do you mean?"

"Us." I gestured between our two bodies. "This." I swallowed hard, emotion tightening my throat. My chest. My soul. "Was any of it real?"

He averted his gaze. "I didn't want it to be."

I squeezed my eyes shut, my heart aching from his frigid tone.

"But hindsight's always twenty-twenty."

I snapped my gaze back to him as he took another timid step toward me.

"I may have had my reasons for doing the things I have, but I meant what I told you the other night. I'm falling for you. And not as Sam, but as Gideon. After the things I was forced to endure..."

The muscles in his face tightened, his expression anguished. He closed his eyes, taking several moments to collect himself. When he returned them to mine, they were filled with so much pain.

"I didn't think I'd ever feel anything but anger. Hate. Rage. For years, my anger was the only thing that helped me survive. But with you..." Tentatively, he reached for my hand.

This time, I didn't recoil from him. Instead, I relished in the feel of his skin on mine, despite the confusion still plaguing me.

"You make it not hurt as much, Imogene. I'm begging you to give me a chance to explain. After that, if you never want to see me again, I'll understand. But don't push me away before you know the truth. I *want* you to know the truth, despite what my actions may have led you to believe."

Since learning who he was, I'd wanted answers. Wanted to know how he could have been alive when the world thought he was dead. Wanted to know how he could lie to me.

Wanted to know who was responsible for turning the man I once loved into someone I barely recognized.

I couldn't shake the feeling I wasn't going to like those answers.

But I needed closure. I'd never truly be able to move on from this with hundreds of questions left unresolved.

"Okay. I'll listen."

He pushed out a relieved breath as his lips curved into a small smile that reminded me so much of Samuel it ached. "Thank you, Imogene."

CHAPTER TWENTY

Gideon

"What would you like to know?" I asked Imogene once we were sufficiently away from the few people gathered at the top of Stone Mountain.

Without even discussing it, we'd both navigated down our usual path of the Cherokee trail. It was a longer hike than the route most people took back, but it was worth the extra few miles to walk along the tree-covered trail, past the creek, and by several Civil War era buildings.

"Everything." She laughed under her breath. "And nothing at the same time, if that makes any sense."

"It makes perfect sense. I want to tell you everything and nothing, too. Not because I don't want you to know,"

I added quickly. "Some of the things I had to go through, Imogene..." I shifted my gaze toward her, meeting her confused stare. "They won't be easy for you to hear, but I want you to know everything. Even if I hate having to relive the worst time of my life."

"What happened? How are you still alive when every expert said you'd never be able to survive that amount of blood loss without immediate medical care?"

I stuffed my hands into the pockets of my shorts. "Because I *did* get immediate medical care, just not in the traditional sense." I looked forward, the sun peeking through the canopy of leaves coupled with the sounds of nature reminding me I was free.

That I'd survived.

That the men who did this to me would soon pay for their crimes.

"I thought it was a good Samaritan. Now I know he was hired to clean up the mess."

"By who?"

I licked my lips and studied her. "What I'm about to tell you might be difficult to hear, and if I didn't think it was necessary, I wouldn't. But it's more dangerous for you *not* to know."

"You're not making any sense, Gideon." She shook her head, then corrected, "Samuel. I don't even know what to call you."

"It's safer if you stick with Gideon."

"Who shot you? Was it Jonah?"

I narrowed my gaze on her. "I think we both know it wasn't."

She blew out a breath, nodding in agreement. "Then who?"

I hesitated briefly, a part of me worried she wouldn't believe me. That she'd choose Liam over me, as she often did during our relationship, thanks to the years he spent manipulating her.

But she needed to know. I could only hope she'd be able to see past years' worth of Liam's mind games to the truth.

"Liam," I said finally, the name seeming to ring out around us.

She came to an abrupt stop, dirt and leaves kicking up around her. Her eyes widened in shock and confusion, her mouth falling open. "Liam? H-how? Why? Are you sure?"

"A lot about that time of my life is a blur. But I'll never forget seeing the man I thought was my best friend and business partner point a gun at me."

"Why? Why would he do that to you?"

"Why do most people commit crimes?" My lips curved into a bitter smile. "Greed. Money."

Realization washed over her, as if the missing piece of a puzzle finally snapped into place. "You were against selling Cloud Hero to ImageScape."

"Without me in the picture, Liam Pierce became one of the richest men in America."

"And this good Samaritan?"

"He was hired to clean up the...mess."

"Mess?"

"My body," I replied bluntly, not sugarcoating anything.

"Oh." She looked forward, her expression becoming more uneasy with every new piece of information. But I couldn't stop here. There was so much more she needed to know.

Not to clear me of my crimes. Nothing could do that.

But to keep her safe.

"When he got there, I was still alive. Instead of killing me, this cleaner — Brian McGuire — decided to make some money off of me."

"How?"

"By patching me up and selling me like a piece of property. Based on what I've learned, he does a lot of this type of cleaning. It's perfect when you think about it. He's a funeral director with a goddamn cremation oven at his disposal. He can easily get rid of any and all evidence. And certain people will pay a premium for that."

I didn't tell her *how* I came about that information, considering I learned it when I went through his things while I waited for his body to be turned to ash last night.

"Who did he sell you to? How could anyone—"

"I don't know who exactly. Henry is still trying to track down exactly who was behind it." I'd hoped I'd find something in Brian McGuire's files, but they were all fairly cryptic, requiring Henry's expertise.

"What did you get sold into?"

"Underground fights. Death matches. Modern-day gladiator fights broadcast on the dark web for anyone willing to pay to watch and place bets on who would survive." Bile rose in my throat from the memory, but I pushed it down, needing to get through this so Imogene could understand my actions.

And the lies I told.

Imogene's face paled as she raked her gaze down my body before meeting my eyes. "That's how you got all the scars."

It wasn't a question. Merely an observation.

"Yes."

She sucked in a shuddering breath, tears welling in her eyes. "How long were you trapped there before you escaped?" she squeaked out.

"Three years, ten months, two weeks, and twenty-eight hours." My voice was heavy with the weight of those years.

"I assume whoever was holding you didn't let you go out of the goodness of his heart."

"You're right about that." A shiver rolled down my

spine as one particular memory of the depravity I'd witnessed returned to the surface.

We'd all been escorted into the training room where one of the newer prisoners knelt handcuffed in the middle of the cage, as I referred to the ring we fought in. He was a decent-sized guy, but he committed the horrible sin of trying to escape.

It wasn't enough for the guards to simply put a bullet in his head. They used every escape attempt as a way to brainwash us into obedience.

For six horrific hours, we were forced to listen to his cries and pleas for help as a pack of dogs tore him apart. But they didn't kill him, as if they were trained that way. It wasn't until the head guard grew bored that he allowed him to be put him out of his misery.

But he wasn't the one to shoot him. Instead, he made one of us do it.

Made *me* do it.

His was the first life I ever took. I'd remember it for the rest of my days.

"How did you escape?" Imogene's voice pulled me out of that pit of death, returning me to the present.

"I got lucky when they were transporting us after a fight. The van hit some rough weather and lost control, crashing into a tree. The driver, guards, and the rest of the prisoners all died. I should have died, too. It's still a blur, but I was able to think clearly enough to use the opportunity to escape.

"We'd been so hardwired against disobedience that they didn't even bother handcuffing or chaining us when we were being transported, which allowed me to make a run for it after I was able to free myself from the smashed van. I had no idea where I was, but I didn't care. I just wanted to get as far away from that van as possible. I was so fucking paranoid. So goddamn scared someone would find me and drag me back there. Every mile was torture, but I knew I couldn't look back."

"Like Orpheus," Imogene remarked softly.

I laughed slightly, meeting her eyes. She was always fascinated by Greek Mythology, and the tale of Orpheus and Eurydice was one of her favorites. It was one of mine, too. A reminder of the perils of always looking behind you and never forward.

Wasn't that what I was doing by carrying out this vendetta?

Wasn't I looking back instead of ahead?

"I eventually stumbled on a cabin by a lake," I continued, shaking off the thought. "With no shoes and only a ratty t-shirt and shorts to protect me from the elements, I wouldn't survive the night if I didn't break in. At that point, my sole focus was on surviving. Not long term, either. I was taking this minute by minute.

"Luckily, I found a key hidden in a fake rock by the front door, so I didn't have to cause any damage. It's funny," I mused to myself. "I'd just spent four years killing to survive, yet I was worried about trespassing on someone's property."

"Because you didn't lose your humanity." She offered me a warm smile I didn't deserve.

"I wouldn't be so sure about that."

She stopped walking, and I did the same. "It's still in there." She placed her hand on my chest. "In here. If it wasn't, you wouldn't have looked as distraught as you did this morning. You wouldn't be standing here right now, telling me the truth."

I shook my head, staring down at her in wonder. "How do you do it?"

"Do what?"

"How do you keep your compassion after everything I did? I've killed people, Imogene."

"I know better than most that sometimes you're forced to do things you never thought you would in order to survive. That's all you did."

I pushed out a sigh and stepped out of her touch. "I wouldn't judge me too kindly yet," I said, continuing along the path.

She may have understood why I took the lives I did while in captivity. But the lives I'd taken since then?

They weren't to survive.

They were out of vengeance, pure and simple. And I didn't regret a single one.

"What happened once you found safety?" she asked after a few moments of silence as we walked along the bubbling brook.

"I didn't want to stay there for too long. Just long enough to eat and clean up, maybe find some clothes. But as I walked into the living room, I caught sight of a mirror. It had been nearly four years since I'd seen my own reflection. At first, I thought I was staring at someone else. I was bigger, sure. But my face... They didn't care if we were injured. I'd suffered a dislocated jaw. Broken nose. Missing teeth. Hell, I was still covered in blood from that night's match. And it wasn't *my* blood, either.

"That was when the reality of everything I'd been through finally hit me. It didn't sink in when the guards tortured me in order to toughen me up for matches. Nor did it sink in the first time I entered that cage and had to kill in order to survive. But that moment, staring at my reflection with someone else's blood staining my skin? It was all too much. All I wanted was to wash it off, as if that would erase what I'd been through. What I'd done. What I'd become."

"Gideon, I..."

"So I took the longest shower I ever had," I cut her off before she could offer me any more words of understanding or comfort. "It probably took a good twenty or thirty minutes before the water ran clear. Afterward, I rummaged through the closet and found some clothes. They were a little snug, but it was better than nothing. Then I..." I trailed off, swallowing hard as I glanced her way.

"Yes?" she prodded gently.

"Then I called you."

CHAPTER TWENTY-ONE

Imogene

My feet skidded to a sudden halt, my eyes widening as I gaped at Gideon. Samuel. Whoever the hell he was.

My thoughts were already a jumbled mess after everything he shared with me. But to learn I was the first phone call Samuel made when he was finally free? It was an even bigger punch to the gut than his claim that Liam shot him, something I still struggled to believe.

"When?" I asked in a shaky voice.

"March third of last year," he responded evenly.

I blinked repeatedly, wracking my brain for a memory of that. If he'd called, that day would have been etched in my mind for the rest of my life.

"Did I answer?"

"Yes."

I hoped he'd tell me I didn't. That I'd sent it to voicemail.

But to learn I'd answered? That I'd spoken to him?

"Hearing your voice again, Imogene," he continued when I remained too stunned by this revelation to formulate a response, "it made everything I suffered worth it."

"Why don't I remember that?"

"Because you accused me of being some asshole playing a prank on you. Called me a heartless prick who deserved to have his balls set on fire."

I clapped a hand over my mouth, remembering that call with clarity now.

Following Samuel's disappearance, I'd fielded all sorts of phone calls. Most were from reporters hoping to interview me for a story about him, since I was such a close friend.

Unfortunately, there were always a few assholes who thought it would be fun to call pretending to be Samuel, especially since his body had never been found. Everyone told me to ignore them, that it wasn't healthy to hold on to hope he was still out there.

The one time it *was* him, I'd chased him off.

"That was you?" I squeaked out.

How different would our lives have been if I hadn't hung up on him? Would he be the same tortured man standing in front of me? Or would I have been able to help him move on from his past?

"That was me." He gave me a sad smile. "I thought about calling back. Then I realized you wouldn't believe me until you looked into my eyes and saw the truth. So I went through the house and found some cash stashed away. I hated stealing, but all I cared about was getting back to Atlanta. Getting back to you."

"Then why didn't you?" I asked, blinking back the tears welling in my eyes.

"I did."

"I would have remembered that. There's no—"

"You were with *him*," he cut in, his voice laced with contempt.

"Who?" I asked, even though I knew all too well who he was referring to.

"Liam. I saw him pull up in front of your townhouse and help you out of his car. Then I saw him walk you up to the door. And then I saw him kiss you. And then I saw you invite him in."

I squeezed my eyes shut, guilt festering in my stomach. Liam was a mistake from the beginning. Now I regretted it more than ever. What must Samuel have thought when he saw us together? Especially with everything he just shared.

"I was so fucking angry, Imogene," he seethed, his jaw clenched and nostrils flaring. "The entire time I was locked up, you got me through it. Yes, the idea of getting out and making Liam and the rest of them pay certainly helped, but when I saw you with the man who shot me? All I thought was that maybe you were part of it, too, especially since I'd been begging you to finally let me tell him about us, and you constantly refused."

I reached for his hand, gently tracing my fingers over the bandages covering his wounds. "I'm so sorry I made you think…" I sucked in a quivering breath as I met his tortured gaze. "It's no excuse, but losing you hurt so damn much. And Liam…"

I looked away, unable to meet his eyes as the guilt for my actions festered in my stomach.

"I always regretted it right after, but feeling something for a few minutes was better than the emptiness that had consumed my life since I learned you died. If I knew you were still alive, I never would have—"

"I know," he interrupted, giving my hand a reassuring squeeze. "Once I started spending time with you and got to know you again, heard you talk about Samuel, I realized I was wrong." He held my gaze for another beat before dropping his hold on me and continuing along the path.

"Why didn't you tell me the truth from the beginning?" I asked once I caught up with him. "Why all the lies?"

"At first, I thought you were just as responsible, even

if you didn't pull the trigger. The fact that you invited Liam into your bed?" His voice trembled, as if merely saying the words caused him unimaginable pain. "I felt betrayed, Imogene. I wanted you to hurt like I did, and I didn't care what it took."

I darted my gaze toward his as another piece of the puzzle clicked into place. "Were *you* behind those necklaces? And the attack in the alley?"

"No," he stated unequivocally.

"You expect me to take you at your word?" I arched a skeptical brow. "That it was a coincidence you just so happened to be at the club when I was attacked?"

This was the hardest part of this whole situation. He'd lied to me since the beginning of our relationship. Or since the beginning of my relationship with Gideon. How was I supposed to believe anything he told me now?

"It *wasn't* a coincidence. I was watching you," he admitted nonchalantly. "When I saw you head out the back door, I knew something was wrong." He stole a glance my way, his expression tight with tension. "I may regret a lot of things where you're concerned, but I don't fucking regret following you into that alley. Not for a goddamn minute, Imogene. When I saw that asshole on top of you..." He trailed off as he squeezed his eyes shut, the anguish on his face reminding me of his expression when he paid me a visit at the hospital following the attack.

I thought it odd for him to be so concerned, since I was a stranger to him.

Or I *thought* I was.

Now it made sense.

"Nothing else mattered except making him pay," he finished with a low growl.

"What about the body of the guy who sent me those necklaces that was found on Liam's boat? Benjamin Astor. Liam claims it was planted to frame him." I paused. "Was that you?"

"No one hurts you and gets away with it, Imogene," he declared with determination. "*No one.*"

I should have been angry that he essentially just admitted to killing a man for me, but I couldn't ignore the thrill that raced through me from his protectiveness. After all, I'm only alive right now because he intervened.

But was one good act enough to erase everything else he did? And making it look like Liam was responsible? I still struggled to wrap my head around his involvement in this, if Gideon was to be believed. I *wanted* to believe him. I just didn't know if I could.

"What about Alton's death?" I asked, needing to think about something else for a minute. "The fingerprints the police found weren't from five years ago, were they?"

He slowly shook his head.

"Why Alton? What does he have to do with any of this?"

"He wanted me gone just as much as Liam did. He bought up a bunch of stock in ImageScape when Liam told him they would soon be acquiring Cloud Hero. At least in *his* mind, they would be. He didn't think anyone would turn down billions of dollars."

"And once he bought up all that stock, Alton stood to lose a fortune if the sale didn't happen."

"Exactly. But being a greedy bastard wasn't the only thing that got him on my list."

"No?"

"He was the one who told the police he saw the gun found near my supposed murder scene in Jonah's backpack just a few days prior. I should have questioned why he suddenly wanted to volunteer when he typically couldn't be bothered. Once I learned that, all the pieces snapped into place. This wasn't a spur-of-the-moment decision. The three of them planned this. Extensively, too. They planned for Liam to kill me. Then hired Brian McGuire to dispose of my body. Then arranged for Jonah to take the blame. Then James made sure he was silenced before he could prove his innocence."

"James?"

"He may be the worst of them all. Not only did he conspire with Brian McGuire to sell me, but when he was a DA, he used his position of authority to broker deals with criminals. Took bribes in exchange for a reduced sentence or dropped charges. Or in certain circumstances, he'd work a deal if they permanently silenced someone on the inside."

"Jonah," I exhaled.

"Exactly."

The flood of information made my head swim. How could I have been so blind to what was happening right under my nose? And at Liam's direction?

Or was all of this a lie, too?

I was so confused.

"Why not go to the police?" I pressed. "Tell them everything."

"I don't exactly have much faith in the justice system," he said with a disdainful smile. "Not when I saw how easily James and Liam were able to manipulate it. You may not agree with it, but I have to do this, Imogene. I need to balance the scales. Not just for me. But for Jonah. I have to make it right for him, too."

I nodded, shifting my eyes forward as I continued walking, my idyllic surroundings at odds with the myriad of thoughts warring for attention in my mind.

"What's your end goal here?" I asked finally, even though I had a feeling I'd regret it.

"You know the famous Confucius saying, don't you?" He swallowed hard, confirming my suspicion that I wouldn't like his response. "'Before you embark on a journey of revenge, dig two graves.'"

I faltered in my steps, and he wrapped an arm around my waist to steady me. "You don't mean—"

"My grave has already been dug, Imogene. It was the second Liam pointed a gun at me and fired. I've just been on borrowed time since then."

My heart dropped, tears blurring my vision as I struggled to comprehend his words. I knew what each meant individually, but strung together? I refused to believe it.

"You're planning on sacrificing yourself?"

"I *am* prepared to die to make sure justice is served, should it come to that."

I shook my head, the weight of this too much for me to bear. I tore away from him and paced the dirt path, feeling like my world was spinning uncontrollably around me.

"What am I supposed to do with all of this? How am I supposed to be okay with you dying all over again?"

"I hope it doesn't come to that. I—"

"And what about everything else?" I threw up my hands in exasperation and stopped in front of him, my eyes on fire. "Am I just supposed to keep it to myself, knowing what you most likely plan to do to James and Liam? What you did to Alton?"

"I won't tell you what to do," he responded evenly.

"If you feel the need to go to the authorities and turn me in, I won't fault you for it. In the beginning, I struggled with this path myself. Unfortunately, I've had to come to terms with some hard truths over the past five years."

"Like what?" I crossed my arms in front of my chest.

"There are no absolutes in life. Black and white? Righteous and immoral? Good and evil? Those things don't really exist. No one is purely good or purely bad. Some people do bad things for good reasons."

"And some do good things for bad reasons," I finished.

"You just have to decide for yourself where my actions fall. I can't do that for you."

"And what am I supposed to do about Liam? I can't ignore him forever."

"He won't hurt you," he assured me. "Ever since I learned he hired those men to send you the necklaces, then kidnap you, I've made sure of that."

"Wait. What?" I snapped my eyes back to his.

How much more could I possibly take before I completely lost it? My entire reality had been shattered in a matter of minutes. And now to learn that Liam was behind those necklaces and the attack, as well?

"Why would he do that? That doesn't make any sense."

"Actually, it makes perfect sense. Did he do or say

anything around that time to try to convince you to do something he wanted?"

I parted my lips, about to answer in the negative when I stopped myself, recalling my recent disagreements with Liam. "He kept citing it as a reason why I wasn't safe living alone," I said under my breath, a heat washing over me. "You don't think he did all of that just so I'd move in with him, do you?" I met his gaze.

"Where you're concerned, nothing's off limits for Liam." He reached for my hand and I allowed him to take it in his. "Regardless of *why* he hired those men, he still put your life in danger. I won't give him a chance to do it again."

"I still can't..." I trailed off, struggling with all the bombs he'd dropped on me in the past several minutes. Hell, since dropping the biggest bomb of all on me this morning.

"I've thrown a lot of information at you." He ran his thumb over my knuckles.

Normally, I'd find the gesture soothing. But nothing could soothe the turmoil swirling inside of me like a tumultuous storm.

"I don't blame you if you have trouble believing me," he continued, able to read my thoughts and reservations. "I haven't exactly given you any reason to trust me, but do me a favor."

"What's that?"

He released my hand, and a chill trickled down my spine from the loss of contact.

"The next time you speak to Liam, mention that a detective reached out and was asking questions about my death."

"You want me to lie to him?"

He blew out a laugh. "Imogene, he's lied to you every time he's pretended to be upset about my death. If you doubt my story, Liam's expression should erase it."

I chewed on my lower lip, shaking my head as I considered his proposition. Then I spun on my heels, storming down the trail.

"You've really fucked with my head here," I remarked bitterly when he caught up with me.

"That was never my intention. At least not since..."

I looked his way, slowing my pace. "Since when?"

"Since I saw your tattoo." A sad smile pulled at the corners of his mouth. "You have no idea how hard it's been not to trace that symbol whenever I've been lucky enough to watch you fall asleep beside me. When I saw that..." His voice wavered with emotion. "That's when I knew."

"Knew what?" I asked through the heaviness in my throat.

He slowed his steps, grabbing my hand and pulling me to a stop. "That you never stopped loving Samuel."

"You know what unconditional means, don't you?" I said with a quiver.

He nodded slowly. "Not based on any conditions or qualifications."

"Absolute," I added.

"Complete." He adjusted his stance, moving closer toward me as I lost myself in his eyes. *Samuel's* eyes.

"Unequivocal," I exhaled.

"Pure."

"I loved you unconditionally, Samuel," I said through my tears, my words barely audible.

"Then I can only hope your unconditional love will help you understand why I've done what I have. Why I need to keep doing what I am. Until then..." He leaned toward me and brushed a soft kiss against my forehead.

I closed my eyes, relishing in the warmth of his lips on my skin, breathing in his familiar scent.

"The ball is in your court, Imogene," he whispered against me. "You can do with it what you think is best."

With one last kiss to my forehead, he released me and turned to walk in the opposite direction.

Ever since learning he was Samuel this morning, I'd wanted the truth. Wanted to know how he could have deceived me like he did.

But the truth only left me more confused about this man who was both a stranger yet still owned a piece of my heart.

CHAPTER TWENTY-TWO

Imogene

I breathed in the cool ocean air as I made my way up the succulent-lined path and onto my front porch, pulling my suitcase behind me.

A few weeks ago, I welcomed the perfect climate here in California, if for no other reason than because it was symbolic of my fresh start.

Now it only served as a reminder this wasn't the fresh start I thought it would be.

Instead, my past followed me here.

I still wasn't sure what to do with the truth about Gideon...Samuel.

I almost wished he hadn't told me. Wished I never knew.

One minute, my heart ached for Gideon.

The next, his story seemed too farfetched to be real.

Did Liam *really* shoot Samuel all because he didn't want to sell Cloud Hero to ImageScape, like Liam wanted? Granted, Gideon's claim that Alton bought up a bunch of stock in anticipation of the sale was certainly believable.

But Liam? A murderer? I still struggled with that.

Hell, I still struggled with everything.

I wanted to believe Gideon, but I couldn't forget all the lies he'd told me. Was all of this yet another lie? Was any of it real, even all those years ago?

How was I supposed to reconcile the man I thought I loved with the man he was now?

With the *killer* he was now?

Approaching the front door, I entered my code into the keypad, wanting nothing more than to crawl into my bed and pretend the past week never happened, if only for a few hours.

But the instant I walked inside, I was greeted with an unexpected reminder of Samuel.

Ollie barreled toward me, his tail feverishly wagging as he jumped up to greet me. All the tears I'd kept at bay since yesterday afternoon rushed forward, especially as I recalled each and every time Gideon had interacted with Ollie.

I said from the beginning that Ollie seemed to take to

him much quicker than any other man. Now I knew why.

Allowing my purse to slide off my shoulder, I dropped to the floor, wrapping my arms tightly around Ollie as he showered me with kisses.

"You knew all along, didn't you? You knew your daddy was still alive."

He barked excitedly, continuing to lick my face.

"And you still forgave him? Didn't care that he'd been gone for years?"

Ollie nuzzled into me almost in apology, his nose wet against my skin.

"I get it," I said with a heavy sigh. "You missed him and were just happy to see him again." I leaned against the wall, extending my legs in front of me, scratching the spot behind his ears he loved. "I wish I could be as happy as you, Ol. I just... I don't know whether to trust him. Or believe him."

I clutched his adorable face in my hands, some of the tan fur around his nose and brow turning white with age.

"Can you tell me what I'm supposed to do? How I can just trust him again?"

For a fraction of a second, I truly believed Ollie was about to impart some pearls of wisdom on me.

Instead, a knock sounded, followed by a familiar voice.

"Ginny? You home?"

Ollie's formerly excited expression fell, and he growled, baring his teeth.

For the first time in all the years I'd known Liam, my reaction sort of mirrored Ollie's.

My pulse quickened, a bout of nerves washing over me at the idea of talking to him after everything Gideon shared with me. I wasn't sure if I could face him without letting on that I knew something.

Then I remembered what Gideon asked of me. That if I had any doubt about his story, all I needed to do was mention the police had reached out regarding Samuel's death. That Liam's reaction would tell me everything I needed to know.

Drawing in a deep breath, I pulled myself to my feet, doing my best to fix my expression into a mask of indifference.

"Liam," I greeted cordially after opening the door and slipping onto the front porch, not inviting him inside as I normally would.

I could only pray he didn't read too much into my demeanor. After all, we hadn't spoken since our argument in Pebble Beach. At least I had that to help explain any changes in my behavior.

"Hey, Gin."

"What are you doing here? I—"

"Is it too late for an apology?" He gave me a sheepish smile, shifting from foot to foot.

It was hard for me to imagine Liam being capable of all the things Gideon accused him of.

But people probably could have said the same about my sperm donor. He was a genius. A well-respected college professor.

Yet that didn't stop him from ending the lives of dozens of innocent women.

Or making my mother's life a living hell for years.

Or kidnapping me and forcing me to witness the worst of humanity.

"An apology?" I crossed my arms in front of my chest and leaned against the exterior siding.

"For the way I behaved in Pebble Beach. I was angry and confused, and I said some things that hurt you. I just care about you, Imogene. That's all. I want what's best for you. And Gideon Saint..."

At the name, I swallowed hard, my pulse kicking up. I hoped he didn't notice my sudden intake of air or the way I fidgeted with my hands.

"I know you have feelings for him," he continued, his jaw clenching. "There may be nothing I can do or say to make you change your mind, but as your friend, I can't just stand aside and remain silent. And it's not out of jealousy or whatever my actions may have led you to believe. It's because I'd never forgive myself if I didn't say something and you ended up like Alton."

"This again? Liam, I—"

"I know." He dug his fingers through his hair in frustration as he paced the short length of my front porch. "But between the attack at the club, the body on my boat, and now Alton's sudden death? There's something going on."

"You're right. I think there *is* something suspicious going on."

He straightened, darting his eyes to mine, obviously surprised by my response.

"You do?"

"Why else would a detective contact me?"

"They...did?" he stammered.

If I didn't know Liam this well, I wouldn't have thought anything of his reaction. But I knew him. Knew his tells. And the way he repeatedly swallowed and blinked told me he was nervous.

"Yesterday."

"About what?"

"Alton's death." I chewed on my lower lip. "Although I guess it was more about Samuel."

His face blanched. "Samuel?"

I nodded. "He asked if I could remember the last time he may have visited Alton's cabin." I feigned confusion. "Do you know why that would matter?"

He forced a smile, but didn't look directly at me. "Your guess is as good as mine."

I knew for a fact Liam was more than aware of why

the police might want to find out the last time Samuel Tate had been at Alton's cabin. That Liam would easily lie about this told me he'd have no problem lying about other things, too.

"He also asked about Samuel's death," I continued when he didn't embellish further.

"He did?"

"He said they may have uncovered some new evidence about what happened to him. To Samuel," I clarified.

"Did he say what this evidence was?"

"Only that it was an ongoing investigation," I replied coolly, a complete juxtaposition to Liam's unease. "Which is why I wanted to ask you. See if you knew anything more."

His Adam's apple bobbed up and down in several more hard swallows, his expression becoming paler by the second.

"Sorry to say I don't. But if I hear anything, I'll be sure to let you know. What did you say this detective's name was?"

I squinted, pretending to wrack my brain.

"I can't remember. You know how bad I am at remembering names."

"Right."

He ran his fingers through his hair for what seemed like the tenth time, then cleared his throat.

"Well, I'll let you get back to your evening. I'm behind on work after everything that's happened, but I wanted to stop by. Make sure you were okay. That *we* were okay. Maybe we can have a movie night sometime soon when life slows down a bit."

"I'd like that."

"Me, too." He leaned down and brushed a kiss on my cheek.

It took everything inside me to keep my cool. But I somehow managed to mask my emotions as if my life depended on it.

In a way, it did.

When Liam finally pulled back and started down the stairs, I rushed inside. His retreating voice sounded from the other side of the door and I moved toward the bay windows, watching him hurry toward his car with his cell glued to his ear, his posture rigid.

I held my breath, straining to listen to what he was saying over the clicking of Ollie's nails against the hardwood floor. I gestured for my dog to come to me, and he eagerly obeyed, allowing me to make out Liam's side of the conversation through the slight opening in my window.

"I'm flying out there tonight," Liam barked into his phone. "We have a problem. Some detective called Ginny and is asking what happened to Sam. You need to fix this. I am *not* going down for his murder."

When he reached his luxury SUV and looked back at my house, I quickly ducked down, not so much as breathing until I heard the familiar sound of his car rumbling down the street.

The reality of everything Liam just confirmed instantly sank in, shattering my world into a million pieces. Liam really did it. He planned to kill his best friend and business partner, then conspired with James and Alton to cover it up.

And being the trusting, naïve girl I'd always been, I never suspected him. In fact, I invited him into my bed. All along, I was sleeping with the person who'd taken away the man I loved.

My entire body shook uncontrollably as my sobs overtook me, a heart-wrenching wail echoing in the house. Sensing my distress, Ollie whimpered beside me, trying to offer comfort in any way he could.

"He did it, buddy," I managed to choke out. "The bastard really did it."

CHAPTER TWENTY-THREE

Imogene

The first rays of morning light filtered through my bedroom window as I stared at the ceiling with weary eyes. After a sleepless night spent replaying every moment of the past several months over and over again, the patterns and swirls on the surface had become etched into my memory.

Exhaustion consumed me, but that did little to dull the ache in my chest. Every time I closed my eyes, I saw Liam's stare. His smile. His deception.

And I fell for it. Allowed him to comfort me after Samuel was presumed dead. Then, on those nights when the pain was too unbearable, I invited him into my bed. He pretended to still mourn his best friend when, all along, he was the reason Samuel was gone.

It sickened me to think how blind I'd been. How *trusting* I'd been. And he used that trust against me, to the point that I was nearly killed in a dark alley because of him. I would have been if Gideon hadn't intervened.

No wonder he seemed like he wanted to murder Liam when he showed up at the hospital after the attack. It was a miracle he didn't. I wouldn't have been able to stomach being in the same room as someone who'd betrayed me like that, causing me to suffer unimaginable horrors.

Gideon may not have gone into detail about what he'd endured, but he didn't have to. I saw the scars that marred his body from years of having to fight for his life — literally — so that a bunch of depraved assholes could profit off him.

The idea made my stomach churn once more, and I rushed into the bathroom, where I dry heaved until there was nothing left inside except bitter resentment and raw hatred.

I splashed cold water onto my face, trying to wash away this awful feeling. Deep circles framed my eyes, a physical manifestation of the turmoil within.

The weight of everything was too much. I needed to get out of here. Clear my mind. Find some sort of peace in a world that was spinning more and more out of control with every second.

I rinsed out my mouth and headed back into my

bedroom, changing into a bikini before slipping into my wetsuit. After tossing a towel and some dry clothes into my bag, I slid on my flip-flops and continued downstairs, grabbing Gertie, my surfboard, on the way.

As I walked the short distance from my townhouse and toward the beach, awareness prickled my nape. It wasn't the same as when I knew Gideon was watching me. This was more chilling, making me feel like a standing target.

I glanced around, looking for something out of the ordinary. But I didn't see anything. No one lurking in the shadows. No suspicious cars. Just a quiet neighborhood in the predawn hours.

Trying to find comfort in Gideon's assurances that he'd made sure Liam couldn't hurt me, I continued down the sandy path, coming to an abrupt stop by The Daily Grind when my gaze fell on a familiar figure sitting at his usual table.

I hadn't seen Gideon since our hike together on Monday. It was Wednesday.

But that hike felt like a lifetime ago now.

Hell, our night together before that seemed like a lifetime ago.

I was a different person back then.

I still thought Samuel was dead. Thought Gideon could be my future. Thought Liam had my best interests at heart, despite our disagreements.

How quickly that all changed.

Now that I knew the truth, I couldn't help but see parts of Samuel in Gideon as we silently stared at each other. Like the way he sipped his coffee. Or the way the corner of his mouth always seemed to twist up on one side whenever he saw me. Or the way the vein in his forehead throbbed whenever he tried to decipher a particularly difficult crossword clue.

These reminders of the man I loved simultaneously broke my heart yet filled it with hope at the same time.

Without either of us saying a word, I turned from him and headed toward the shore. The early morning light painted the ocean in shades of pink and orange, casting a serene glow on the waves. After dropping my bag on the sand, I attached the tether to my ankle, then set my board on the water and paddled out.

Even though I tried to brace myself for the chilly temperatures of the west coast waters, it still sent a shock through my body as I plunged in.

Regardless, the frigid ocean revitalized me. Reminded me I was alive.

Once I paddled to just past where the waves broke, I pushed myself into a sitting position, my legs dangling on either side of the board. Closing my eyes, I took a deep breath and let myself sway with the gentle rhythm of the ocean. There was something so soothing about disconnecting from reality and surrendering to the movements of the unforgiving sea, allowing it to guide me wherever it pleased. I couldn't control it. All I could do was adapt.

Sort of like this situation with Gideon.

No matter how much I wished I could change what had transpired, it was impossible. All I could do was go with the flow, make the best decision for me based on my current circumstances. Not what I wished could be.

I opened my eyes and let my gaze wander toward the shoreline, drawn to the lone figure sitting outside of The Daily Grind. Despite the lies, despite the deception, despite the betrayal, I felt comfort with the knowledge that Gideon was watching me.

Shouldn't that count for something?

Shouldn't that count for *everything*?

Shifting my attention away from him and back to the horizon, I saw a wave building in the distance. The timing seemed perfect as it steadily approached. Flattening my stomach against the board, I began paddling and hoisted myself onto my feet when it crested beneath me, a grin tugging on my lips as I moved with the swells.

After the past few days, I didn't think anything could make me smile, but something about surfing had always helped center me.

During those few moments of utter terror and absolute bliss as I rode a wave into shore, I didn't think of anything else. Not about Gideon. Or Samuel. Or Liam. It was just me, my board, and the ocean.

Which was why, once I reached the sand, I grabbed my board and paddled out yet again, savoring in the invigorating sensation of the salty water on my face and the cool breeze ruffling through my hair.

After riding a few more waves into shore, I needed to get ready for work, especially since the sky was now more day than night.

I peeled out of my wetsuit and tugged on a pair of shorts before trudging back up the sand with my board.

Despite my longer than normal surfing session this morning, Gideon still sat at his usual table. And like before, his only acknowledgment of my presence was a small nod of his head, which I returned.

He told me the ball was in my court. He obviously meant it.

I started past him, but paused, facing him once more. I opened and closed my mouth several times, struggling to find the words I needed. There was so much I wanted to tell him. So much he deserved to hear.

But instead of getting inundated with all of that, I stuck with what I felt was the most important.

"I believe you."

My words echoed in the peaceful air, wrapping around both of us in a protective cocoon. The weight he'd been carrying physically evaporated as he basked in my statement.

He lifted his gaze toward mine, striking blue to dark

brown. Then his deep voice cut through the still morning air. "Thank you."

He didn't say anything else. Didn't make any move toward me. Didn't take my belief in him to mean anything more than it was.

Because I wasn't sure if it *could* mean anything more.

Not when I knew he was on what could very well turn into a suicide mission.

I'd already lost Samuel once.

I wouldn't survive losing him again.

CHAPTER TWENTY-FOUR

Gideon

"Harder," I demanded as I tensed my muscles, bracing for Henry's assault. I held my breath, waiting for his fist to connect with my stomach.

With a grunt, he delivered another harsh blow, sending waves of agony through me. But I refused to give in, even as nausea threatened to overtake me.

"Again," I gritted out, my voice strained but determined.

"Gideon, man, I don't—"

"Again, Henry."

He pushed out a sigh and shook his head, concern etched on his face. But being the good friend he was, he gave me what I needed, thrusting his mitt-covered hand into my stomach once more, this time with even more force.

I stumbled back, fighting to stay upright as another shock of pain spiraled through me. Henry reached out to steady me, but I pushed him away.

There would be no one to help me to my feet when it mattered. I couldn't have him act like a crutch now. I needed to do this. Needed to build up my strength. Needed to push myself to my limits. *Past* my limits.

"Again," I ordered hoarsely, my throat raw from the exertion. I widened my stance and braced for his attack yet again.

Despite his obvious reluctance, he followed through with another powerful punch.

But this time, I could no longer hold it in. I doubled over, emptying the contents of my stomach into the bucket I kept nearby.

"Okay. We're done now," Henry declared, yanking on the tape securing his boxing gloves to his hands with his teeth before removing them.

"Yeah." I collapsed onto the mat, heaving through the pain. "We're done."

"You're a goddamn sadist." He handed me a water bottle and helped me into a sitting position, propping my back against the wall before lowering himself beside me.

"Just trying to be prepared." I brought the water to my mouth, wincing slightly as I sipped.

Every muscle in my body screamed in protest, but I'd be fine later. Henry may not have understood why I felt the need to subject myself to such brutal abuse, but it wasn't just about being strong physically.

It was about being strong mentally, too.

This was where I fell short, especially after everything I'd endured. Sometimes all it took was a smell to bring me back to that cage. I couldn't have that. Not with what was on the line.

"How are things?" Henry asked after several silent moments.

I knew him well enough to know he wasn't asking to make small talk.

He wanted to know how things were with Imogene now that I'd told her the truth.

"I think she's still processing everything."

"It's better than her turning you in." He passed me a sideways glance. "Do you think she'll turn you in?"

I bent my legs, resting my forearms on my knees. "I don't think so." I ran a towel over my sweat-dampened face. "I went to the beach this morning."

"I figured you would."

"I like my routine."

After my escape, my routine was the only thing that got me from one day to the next. It gave me structure. Helped to prevent me from retreating into the dark recesses of my mind. If I could just get to the next waypoint of my day, I'd be okay.

"Did you talk to her?" Henry asked.

"No."

He blew out a long breath and took a long pull from his water, sweat dripping from his dark hair and landing on the mat.

"But she talked to me."

He darted his gaze toward mine. "What did she say?"

"She believes me."

A small smile tipped on my lips from the memory of hearing those three little words escape her mouth.

I thought hearing her tell me she loved me was the best thing I'd ever hear her say. I was wrong.

"I knew she'd eventually come around." He gave my shoulder a gentle squeeze. "Don't forget. *I* had trouble believing you in the beginning, too. Not that I think you'd lie to me, but your story is fucking intense. Granted, I'd seen some horrible shit during my time in the military, but Imogene... I can only imagine how difficult it must have been for her to learn what you went through."

"It was," I admitted, recalling the tears she shed for me when I shared this part of myself with her.

"Did she tell you what changed her mind?"

"No, but my guess is Liam."

He straightened, furrowing his brows. "Liam?"

I slowly nodded. "When she wasn't sure whether she could believe me after all my lies, I told her to mention to Liam that a detective was asking her questions about my death, then watch his reaction. Considering he paid her a visit yesterday, I assume she did as I asked, and his response was enough for her to realize I was telling the truth."

"So that explains it," he exhaled, shifting his eyes forward.

"Explains what?"

"Last night, Liam took a last-minute trip to D.C. Which is where James Turner is at the moment, although he hasn't shown up to any senate hearings or to his office. But he *has* made a few more calls to a burner phone belonging to a certain funeral director. Apparently, he doesn't like the way his previous meeting ended."

"I'm not sure Brian McGuire is in a position to schedule a follow-up." I flashed a devilish smirk before schooling my expression. "Has anyone alerted the police to his disappearance?"

"Not yet, but it's only a matter of time." He paused, lowering his voice, even though we were alone. "Are you ready for when they do?"

"Of course," I replied confidently, already working up the next steps in my mind.

"This will put James on edge. Possibly Liam, too."

"Good. Let them worry their perfect lives are about to be shattered into pieces. Because that's exactly what's going to happen."

"So nothing's changed, then?" He arched a single brow.

"Why would it?"

"I thought with Imogene finding out the truth you'd—"

"I'd what? Change my mind about this?"

He gave a small shrug of his shoulders. "I thought maybe you'd realize there are more...important things."

"What could be more important than making these assholes pay?"

"Love."

"Love," I scoffed, somehow managing to raise myself to my feet, despite the soreness in my muscles. "That's rich coming from a guy who gets a boner every time he sees his assistant, but refuses to do anything about it."

"I'm just trying to be a decent person." He pushed up to stand. "What's your excuse?"

"My excuse? You want to know what my excuse is?" I advanced on him, my face less than a breath away. "You're looking at it, Henry. You look at it every damn day. I lost who I was because of those assholes. I had to become something I absolutely abhor because of them. Look at these scars," I bellowed, holding my arms wide and doing a slow turn so he was forced to look at the marks on my flesh, even though he'd seen them all before. "Each one represents a life I had no choice but to end. I've lived with their blood on my hands for too damn long."

"You're not to blame." His eyes flickered over the scars with sadness and understanding. "You did what you had to in order to survive."

"I know that. But I can't walk away now, Henry. You claimed you wanted these bastards to pay, too."

"That was before."

"Before what?" I seethed.

"Before Imogene," he said calmly, despite my anger. "Before she made you human again. Sure, I'd love to make these bastards suffer." He approached me, placing a hand on my shoulder. "But I'd rather *you* find peace. And maybe you can have that again with Imogene."

I parted my lips, but no words came.

Could I have that again with Imogene? Could I find peace, knowing those responsible for the hell I was forced to live hadn't suffered as I had?

For the past five years, revenge was the only thing that kept me going. It gave me purpose after everything had been stolen from me.

Without my vendetta, I didn't know who I was.

Shaking my head, I lifted my eyes toward Henry. "I have to do this," I insisted through a tight voice.

Then I spun from him, feeling like I was losing more and more control with every passing day.

CHAPTER TWENTY-FIVE

Imogene

I heaved my exhausted body out of the driver's seat of my SUV and stumbled up the front steps of my townhouse late Saturday afternoon, the weight of the past week heavy on my shoulders.

They say the truth will set you free.

In my case, the truth felt like a burden.

Ever since Liam all but admitted to shooting Samuel, I couldn't focus on anything else. My mind constantly wandered back to our years-long friendship, replaying certain moments through a new lens.

A more *jaded* lens.

And with every resurfaced memory, I wanted to kick myself for not seeing the warning signs that had been so obvious. If only I hadn't allowed the guilt I felt for the role my sperm donor played in his mother's death to cloud my rationale, maybe I would have seen it all sooner. Maybe I could have prevented what happened to Samuel.

The only time I'd felt any sort of peace had been when I was out on the ocean or running along the beach. Even though we hadn't spoken since I told him I believed him, Gideon continued to show up and sit at his usual table at The Daily Grind every day.

I'd begun to crave the early morning hours because I knew I'd see him, despite the confusion and turmoil plaguing me.

If I could just get through the night, I'd find some peace in the morning.

I punched my code into the door and let myself into my house, wishing I hadn't promised Melanie I'd drive up to LA to spend the weekend with her after today's game. So much had happened since the last time I saw her, and I didn't know how to explain it all.

One thing was certain. It wasn't a conversation we could have over the phone. Which was why I'd offered to drive up to see her.

Now, it was the last thing I wanted to do.

Tossing my keys onto the entryway table, I was surprised Ollie wasn't here to greet me, especially since it was dinnertime.

"Ollie. Come on, pal. You hungry? You need to eat before we hit the road."

I stepped into the kitchen and scooped some of his kibble into his bowl.

But even after hearing the telltale sound of his food being poured, he didn't come out from one of his many napping spots.

"Ol?" I called out again, my worry increasing by the minute.

I headed toward my office, since that was where he tended to sleep during the day. When I didn't find him there, I made my way up to his other favorite napping spot — my bedroom.

The instant I crossed the threshold, my heart dropped to the pit of my stomach.

Ollie lay on the floor beside his bed, as if he'd fallen off. His chest rose and fell in a rapid pattern, his eyes wide and mouth agape.

"Ollie?" I scrambled toward him, instinctively running my hand along his side. His heart raced out of control, each inhale a struggle. "What's wrong, pal?"

But he didn't respond or acknowledge me. Instead, he stared straight ahead, confused and disoriented.

Panic seized me, and I bolted downstairs to grab my phone, calling the only person I could think of.

"Imogene," Gideon answered as I returned to Ollie and knelt in front of him, tears streaming down my face.

I opened my mouth to speak, but no words came.

"Imogene?" he repeated, his concern evident. "What's wrong?"

"It's Ollie," I finally managed to choke out.

"Ollie?" His voice cracked on his name.

I knew this man better than most people. Or, I knew *Samuel* better than most people.

I never heard this level of raw fear in his voice before.

"He... I don't know," I rushed out. "I came home, and he was on the floor. His breathing is labored. His pulse is increased. I just—"

"Henry, find the closest vet and call them," he ordered without hesitation. "Tell them we're bringing in a dog that needs to be seen right away." Then he returned his attention to me. "I'll be right there, Imogene," he soothed. "It'll be okay."

"There's no time," I sobbed. "I need to take him in now."

"I'm already here. Let me in."

A knock sounded, echoing through my home.

I straightened, not immediately moving. I wasn't sure I wanted to know why he was already at my house.

Then again, he admitted he'd been watching me for weeks. While a part of me felt it a huge invasion of privacy, I shouldn't have been surprised. After all, this was a man who'd killed to keep me safe. Knowing what I now did about Liam, Gideon wouldn't have left me unprotected. He promised me as much.

Jumping to my feet, I ran down the stairs and opened the door for him.

Unlike the suit he wore earlier this morning, he was now dressed in a pair of sweats and a hoodie, much like Samuel used to wear whenever he came from wrestling practice or the gym.

"Where is he?" he asked with a subtle tremble.

"In my bedroom."

He ran up the stairs, taking them two at a time, and I followed.

During the short time I'd known him as Gideon Saint, he rarely showed much emotion, apart from a few isolated incidents.

But when his vision landed on Ollie, something cracked inside him, the fissure allowing more of Samuel to escape.

"Oh, god," he whispered as he hurried toward him, carefully scooping him into his arms and cradling him. "It'll be okay, buddy. I'm here." He pressed a soft kiss to his head. "You're going to be okay. I promise."

He held him for a moment, inhaling a deep breath. Then he stood, carrying him out of the room and down the stairs, murmuring sweet words of encouragement every step of the way.

When we emerged onto the front porch, Henry

stood outside an idling SUV with the rear passenger door already open. I slid in before Gideon climbed in beside me.

Throughout the short ride to the vet, Gideon clutched Ollie tightly to his chest, begging him to hold on as tears welled in his eyes.

And like that fissure in Gideon's hard exterior allowed a piece of Samuel to escape, seeing this side of him again caused the wall around my heart to crack a little, too.

CHAPTER TWENTY-SIX

Gideon

"Poisoned?" I repeated, a mixture of anger and despair twisting my insides. The lump in my throat felt like a boulder, making it nearly impossible to breathe. "There must be some mistake. How—"

"It's fairly common," Dr. Albright, the veterinarian at a nearby emergency clinic, informed me with a sympathetic look. "All it takes is for a dog to mistake a puddle on the driveway for water, but in reality, it's antifreeze."

"I don't even own antifreeze," Imogene interjected, her voice strained.

Over the past several hours, I'd never seen her cry so damn much.

It made me wonder if this was how she reacted when she'd learned about my supposed death.

It was probably ten times worse.

"And Ollie's never been allowed in the garage," Imogene continued, desperation creeping into her voice. As if that would change what happened to Ollie. "He stays in the house, except when I take him for a walk."

"At Ollie's weight, it wouldn't have taken more than a few tablespoons for the toxins to do some serious damage. He could have consumed that in a small puddle he thought was water."

"Is there something you can give him?" I demanded, digging my fingers through my hair. "An...an antidote. Something? Anything?" I pleaded with her.

"There was."

"Was?" My throat closed up.

"If he was brought in immediately after ingesting the antifreeze, we could have given him something to counteract the effects. But that antidote has a very short window of effectiveness, especially with the levels of poison found in Ollie's bloodstream. With the way the body responds to ethylene glycol, you may not know your dog has ingested it until a day or two later. Dogs may be lethargic at first, then they'll eventually recover, making you think nothing's wrong. Which is when the poison is doing irreversible damage."

"Irreversible?" Imogene squeaked out, her panicked eyes looking between the vet and me. "What does that mean?"

"The poison has attacked his kidney." She turned her laptop toward us, displaying two x-rays, side-by-side. "This is what a normal kidney looks like." She circled the organ on one of the x-rays. "And this is the current condition of Ollie's kidney." She pointed to the same location on the other x-ray.

The differences were glaringly obvious. Ollie's kidney was easily double the size of a normal one, and my heart ached with what he was enduring right now.

"Have you noticed him struggling to relieve himself?" she asked.

"I was at work," Imogene answered. "My pet sitter said he didn't seem interested in eating, but..." She trailed off, her emotions overtaking her again before she choked out, "I thought it was just because he's getting older and slowing down a bit."

"It's not your fault." I wrapped an arm around her and kissed the top of her head, inhaling her familiar scent of coconut and pineapple before addressing the vet. "What can we do? Where do we go from here?"

"I have him on morphine right now to control the pain. At this point, the main concern is quality of life." She hesitated, pinching her lips into a tight line as a look of sympathy crossed her expression. "I'm sorry to say that there's just no quality of life left for poor Ollie. The longer the poison has time to wreak havoc on his system, the more damage it will do and the more pain it will cause him. The humane thing would be—"

"To let him go," I finished, unsure how I was even able to say the words through the ache consuming me.

Imogene clutched me even tighter, her tears moistening my t-shirt.

"I wish there was something more I could do for your sweet boy, but there isn't. The poison has already caused too much damage for his little body to handle. I can have Ollie brought into another room so you can spend some time with him."

I drew in a deep breath and nodded, my heart heavy. "Thank you."

"Of course. And again, I'm sorry." She offered one last sympathetic smile, then slipped into the hallway, closing the door behind her.

"It's all my fault," Imogene sobbed the second we were alone. "I wasn't there for him. How did he even—"

"It is *not* your fault." I cupped her cheeks and forced her eyes to mine, needing her to see the truth in my words. "You did more for that sweet dog than anyone else." I swallowed hard, my own emotions betraying me. "You gave him a home when I couldn't anymore."

"He was all I had left of you." Her voice caught, the raw pain in her words almost more than I could handle. "I couldn't lose him, too."

"He's had thirteen amazing years, Imogene. Dogs

don't live nearly long enough. I wish they did. If I could trade my life for his, I'd do it in a heartbeat. But I can't. It's just... It's his time."

She squeezed her eyes shut, her body trembling through her sobs. It was taking everything I had not to break down with her. I wanted to. Wanted to punch and scream and yell and curse whoever did this to my sweet, innocent boy. He didn't deserve this. He deserved to run after seagulls on the beach in the morning. Deserved to be spoiled with all the pup cups from The Daily Grind he could stomach. Deserved to chase tennis balls in the ocean.

Not be poisoned.

A knock sounded on the door, and Imogene pulled away from me, wiping her cheeks as a petite woman in navy blue scrubs walked in.

"I can show you to the comfort suite, if you're ready."

I doubted we'd ever be ready to say goodbye to Ollie, but I stood anyway, helping Imogene to her feet. "Thank you."

I kept my arm wrapped around her as we followed the woman into another room, this one a stark contrast to the sterile exam room we were just in, the lighting low and the walls painted in muted grays. Soft music played, a candle lit on a nearby table giving the space a calming atmosphere. And in the middle lay Ollie on an oversized dog bed with a shaved patch of skin on his belly and arm, an IV attached.

His eyes were open, but there was no spark left in them. Every so often, a faint whimper escaped his throat, a heartbreaking sound that made my chest squeeze.

"You can take as long as you'd like," the vet tech said. "When you're ready, press this and we'll come in." She gestured to a small button by the door.

"Thank you."

With a subtle nod, she retreated, leaving us alone with Ollie.

"Do you mind if I have a minute with him?" I met Imogene's red-rimmed eyes. "You can stay," I added quickly. "I just wouldn't mind telling him a few things, if you're okay with it."

"Of course," she replied, her chin trembling. "He was your dog first."

I gave her hand a gentle squeeze before releasing her and lowering myself next to Ollie, wrapping my fingers around his paw.

Resting my forehead on his, I breathed in his familiar scent. It killed me to keep my distance for the past year. Every time I saw him with Imogene, I wanted nothing more than to go up to him. Now I regretted that I didn't. I'd never get that time back.

"Hey, boy," I murmured, scratching the spot behind his ears he always loved. But today, he barely acknowledged it. "I know you hurt, so I won't make you suffer much longer. I just wanted to thank you for being there for your mama when I couldn't. For taking care of her all these years. I'll never be able to repay you for looking out for her. You were the best boy ever, and I'm sorry we couldn't have more time together. I thought..." I licked my lips, shaking my head.

"I don't know what I thought, to be honest. Maybe that once this was all over, things could go back to the way they were. I'm sorry I took you for granted." I stole a glimpse at Imogene, her tears falling even harder now. But she still managed to meet my gaze. "Both of you." I held her stare, then pressed my forehead to Ollie's once more.

"I'll never forget you," I whispered, hating that this would be the last time I'd ever feel his soft fur. Ever hear his gentle breathing. Ever smell his awful breath. "I love you, buddy. Now have fun chasing all the seagulls over the rainbow bridge." I held him for a few more moments, fighting back my tears. Then I gave him one last kiss before standing.

As Imogene approached, I started to step away, but she darted out her hand, pulling me back down to the floor beside her. Wrapping her arms around Ollie's frail body, she pressed her face into his fur.

"Thanks for everything, buddy," she strained to say. "For always knowing when I was having a bad day. For always being there for me. For making it easier when I missed him so damn much I didn't think I'd survive."

I pinched my lips together to stop my chin from quivering, a few tears finally escaping.

"But we got through it together. I'm going to miss having you shower me with kisses whenever I get home, even if I was only gone a few minutes. Going to miss watching you try to run after seagulls, even though we both know you're never going to catch one. I'm even going to miss your stinky farts after I let you eat a burger."

"Those were always the worst," I remarked with a low chuckle, remembering that all too well.

"Yes, they were." She laughed through her tears, wiping at her cheeks. Then she returned her attention to Ollie, her expression becoming pained once more. "But most of all, I'm going to miss your love. It was..."

She shook her head, as if searching for the right word. Then she glanced my way, holding my gaze captive.

"Unconditional. A love like that...It doesn't happen often. Thank you for showing me what that was like."

She reached for my hand, our fingers interlocking.

And that was how they stayed as we spent a few more minutes with Ollie.

As we said our final goodbyes.

As we watched him take his last breath.

CHAPTER TWENTY-SEVEN

Imogene

Silence settled like a heavy blanket over the car as Henry drove away from the animal clinic, minus one furry, slobbery passenger. I still had trouble wrapping my head around the idea that Ollie was gone.

But like I reminded myself as we said goodbye, it was the humane thing to do. If we kept him alive, he'd only suffer more.

It didn't make it hurt any less, especially after losing him so unexpectedly, and due to poison. It was going to take me some time to get over this loss.

I was pretty sure it would take Gideon some time, too.

Over the past few hours, I saw more pieces of the old Samuel.

As he clutched Ollie to his chest.

As he kissed his head.

As he told him what a good boy he was.

That wasn't Gideon Saint. It was Samuel. *My* Samuel.

The car finally slowed to a stop, and I looked out the window, expecting to be in front of my townhouse.

But we weren't.

Instead, Henry pulled through an ornate metal gate and up a long drive toward one of the massive beach-front homes I often ran by.

"Where are we?" I asked, confused.

"My place," Gideon answered.

"What are we doing here? I thought—"

He took my hand in his, brushing his thumb along my knuckles. After losing Ollie, I needed his touch. Craved it.

"Ollie was poisoned, Imogene. I don't think it was a coincidence it happened right after you mentioned to Liam that a detective had been looking into my death."

"You think Liam poisoned Ollie?" I asked, feeling like I was going to be sick.

Not because I didn't think he could do something like this. But because the idea was no longer as far-fetched as it once would have been.

"I could be wrong, but something tells me this wasn't

a fucking accident," he replied with a hard edge to his voice. "You can be damn sure I'm not taking any chances with your safety, regardless of how you feel about me right now. So you're going to stay here tonight. You'll have your own space," he added quickly. "Henry's already arranged for someone to install a state-of-the-art security system at your place tomorrow. This time, do *not* give anyone the passcodes. Not even Melanie. No one but you should know them. Okay?"

I swallowed hard at the intensity in his gaze.

While I hated the idea of being forced out of my home, I wasn't sure if I could walk in the front door and not burst into tears at the reminder that Ollie was no longer there to greet me. That I'd never hear his paws scampering on the hardwood floor. That I'd no longer be woken up by his stinky breath as he slobbered all over my face.

"Okay," I finally said with a nod.

"Thank you." He squeezed my hand.

Henry pulled the SUV into the oversized garage, and Gideon jumped out, hurrying to my side to help me to my feet.

"Sorry about Ollie," Henry said, approaching me and wrapping me in a hug. "He was an amazing dog."

"Yes, he was."

He gave me one last squeeze before dropping his

hold on me and looking at Gideon. "I'll head over to her place early with the crew."

"Thanks, brother."

The two men embraced briefly. Then Henry made his way toward the door at the back of the garage.

"He stays in the guest house by the pool," Gideon explained, answering the question plastered on my face. "At least for now."

"I see," I replied, unsure what else to say. I had dozens of questions about Henry's involvement in Gideon's plan for revenge, but I was too exhausted to get into any of that tonight.

"Come on. You've had a long day." His hand was warm and firm on my back as he guided me up the short flight of stairs leading into the house.

He punched a code into the keypad before placing a finger on the scanner. With a click, the door unlocked, and he steered me into the darkened interior of his home, entering yet another code into the panel on the wall beside the garage door. Once he disarmed the security system, he returned his hand to my lower back and led me into an open dining and living space, floor-to-ceiling windows revealing a stunning view of the moonlit ocean.

"This place..." I began, turning a slow circle as I took in my surroundings. "It looks familiar."

Gideon chuckled under his breath. "Liam hoped to buy it. When I found that out—"

"You outbid him."

"I didn't want him living so close to you," he explained casually, as if it were completely normal for someone to spend millions of dollars on a house just to prevent someone else from buying it.

"How do you have so much money?" I blurted out before I could stop myself.

He studied me for a protracted beat, as if weighing what to tell me.

"From what I remember, after your death, your ownership interest in Cloud Hero went to Liam."

His jaw ticked, but he eventually nodded. "It did."

"Right, so…"

"I invested in Henry's company early on. After I showed up on his doorstep, he paid me for my ownership interest."

"And all the talk about being a venture capitalist?"

"Oh, but I am."

With a wink, he walked over to the refrigerator and grabbed a bottle of water, loosening the cap before handing it to me. It was something Samuel always did for me. I couldn't help but smile at the idea that, despite his argument to the contrary, there were still parts of Samuel inside him.

Even if they were buried far below the surface.

"Come on. I'll show you around," he offered, escorting me out of the living area.

He gave me a brief tour of the library, game room, and movie theater on the lower level before heading up to the second floor, where all of the bedrooms were.

As beautiful as the house was, it lacked personality. All the artwork adorning the walls was impersonal, making this place feel more like a museum than a home. Even Liam's many residences had personal touches, mostly in the form of photos of him posing with various notable people, along with a few of us together.

But Gideon had nothing in this house that gave me a clue as to who he truly was. The entire building felt hollow, devoid of personal connection or memories. A pristine façade desperately struggling to conceal the past.

"I had Henry bring some of your things here," Gideon stated as he led me into yet another bedroom decorated with a sophisticated beach vibe.

This one was much more luxurious and expansive than the others, although they were all spacious in their own right. A massive bed stood in the center of the room, draped with a pristine white duvet and decorative pillows in various hues of blue and coral. There was even a reading nook with a large wingback chair and a perfect view of the ocean. I could picture myself curled up in that spot with a good book and a glass of wine, watching as the sun disappeared beyond the horizon.

As I padded across the lush carpeting and toward even more floor-to-ceiling windows, a partition slid open.

"If you ever want to go out onto the balcony, just click this." Gideon pointed to a panel by the bed. "It will open the door for you."

I nodded and stepped onto the terrace, drawing in a deep breath of the briny ocean air. "It's beautiful."

"Yes, it is," Gideon replied. But when I stole a glance at him, his gaze wasn't focused on the horizon. It was glued to me.

The heat in his stare reminded me of the way he looked at me all those years ago.

Of the way *Samuel* looked at me all those years ago.

I turned toward him, my eyes tracing over the face that was foreign yet familiar at the same time. The atmosphere crackled with electricity as I stepped closer, my gaze never straying from his.

But before I could erase the final space separating us, he took a step back and cleared his throat.

"You should get some sleep. If you need anything, I'll be right across the hall."

"Samuel, I—"

"I told you," he cut me off, all traces of the man I fell in love with years ago disappearing in a heartbeat. "It's Gideon."

He turned sharply, his posture rigid and straight as he strode through the room and into the hallway.

The second he disappeared behind the door, I exhaled a long sigh, trying to push down the confusion swirling inside me from his abrupt departure. Maybe I should have insisted on staying at my place, regardless of the memories of Ollie that would surround me.

After dragging myself back inside and closing the doors, I moved toward the ottoman at the foot of the bed where my suitcase rested. I quickly changed into a t-shirt and pair of sleep shorts, then padded across the room toward a door I assumed led to the ensuite bathroom.

Instead, I found myself in a massive closet, bigger than my entire bedroom. Dozens of pristine suits lined the walls, each of them identical to the ones I'd seen Gideon wear over the past few weeks. Why would his suits be in here? Was this *his* bedroom?

I headed toward the dresser along the far wall of the closet and opened one of the drawers. As expected, it contained the same brand of boxer briefs he preferred, all but confirming this was his closet.

But why?

Why would he have me sleep in here when there were a handful of other rooms he could have offered?

Maybe he just wanted to make sure I was comfortable after tonight so he gave me the most luxurious room in the house. Still, I didn't want to impose. Didn't want him to feel like I was kicking him out of his bedroom.

Frowning, I closed the drawer and slipped out of the closet, not stopping until I stood in front of the door to his room. Or the room where he said he'd be sleeping tonight.

"Gideon," I called out as I knocked. "You didn't need to give up your bedroom for me. I'm going to sleep in one of the other rooms, but I wanted to let you know first so you wouldn't get worried."

I paused, waiting for his response, but none came. I pressed my ear up to the door, straining to listen for any movement from within, hearing nothing.

"Gideon?" I called out again, testing the doorknob with a gentle hand.

To my surprise, it gave way, and I tentatively pushed open the door, stepping into another luxurious bedroom, if a bit smaller than the others and without an ocean view. It was darker and colder, the windows covered with blackout curtains. Regardless, there was no sign of Gideon.

I was about to head back into the hallway to continue my search for him when a partially open door caught my attention. If the bedside lamp wasn't illuminated, casting a subtle glow on the space, I probably wouldn't have noticed it. But the cement floor and plywood walls seemed out of place compared to the plush carpeting and lavish furnishings in the room.

Stepping closer, I placed my hand on the door and pushed it wider, taking in the room that resembled a bleak prison cell.

If I didn't know better, I would have assumed Gideon was just having this space remodeled.

But I knew better.

Especially when my eyes fell on the threadbare blanket on the floor beside a framed picture of us, making me all but certain this was where Gideon actually slept at night.

CHAPTER TWENTY-EIGHT

Imogene

I stared at the blades of the ceiling fan, my eyes growing blurry as I watched each hypnotic circle. I'd have given anything for even a minute of rest. But despite my utter exhaustion, sleep still evaded me. Every time I closed my eyes, all I saw was that cell-like closet Gideon slept in.

As much as I wanted to hate him for deceiving me in such a hurtful way, it was becoming increasingly diffi-cult. The more I learned about what he'd endured, the more I saw how it still tormented him, the harder it became to hold on to that anger.

Unsure I could stomach spending another sleepless night staring at the ceiling, I threw the duvet off me and slipped out of the bedroom, hoping to distract myself with a movie or a book.

Everything was eerily quiet as I padded down the stairs, making me wonder if Gideon was even here. I hadn't so much as heard his footsteps in the hallway since his abrupt departure earlier.

But as I turned the corner into the kitchen and found the French doors open to the terrace, I came to an abrupt stop.

It wasn't just the fact that Gideon stood shirtless on the terrace, his head bowed, his muscular arms corded as he leaned against the railing.

It was all the scars marring his body.

I'd seen them before.

But this was the first time I saw them knowing he was Samuel, the reality of everything he'd endured staring back at me. He'd told me the stories. I'd even stumbled upon where he slept. But this... This was when it all truly sunk in. His past was no longer an abstract notion, a horror story he told to justify his actions.

It was real.

Sensing my presence, he straightened and faced me, his piercing gaze locking onto mine. Yet he made no move toward me.

On a hard swallow, I took a slow step in his direction, then another, the ocean breeze causing a chill to trickle down my spine.

I was no longer thinking. Just feeling.

Maybe this was what I should have done all along.

When I was mere inches away, I timidly raised my hand, stopping just short of a jagged scar along his abdomen.

Answering the question on my face, he nodded his permission.

With trembling fingers, I brushed them along the same scar I felt when he first allowed me to see this side of him.

What was going through his mind back then? He may have lied to me about how these scars came to be, but he still shared this piece of himself.

A piece that must have brought forward horrific memories.

Yet he still allowed me to see them.

"How?" I asked in a shaky voice, desperate to know the provenance of each and every mark on his body. To truly understand the depths of his torment.

He didn't say anything right away, just stared at me, his eyes clouded with turmoil. Then he blew out a sigh, his head giving a subtle bob of acceptance.

"A knife slashed me during one of the many fights I was forced to be in," he finally said, his voice thick with unease. It was a shift from the normally confident man I thought him to be.

But it wasn't weakness I heard, even if his words weren't as steady and determined as normal.

Instead, all I heard was the strength he had no choice but to exhibit every day in order to survive.

"When it was either kill or be killed," he added.

I briefly squeezed my eyes shut, swallowing back the tears wanting to fall. But if he could withstand such brutality day after day, I could endure hearing about it, regardless of how much it made me want to scream at the unfairness of it all.

Holding his gaze, I gradually leaned down and touched a soft kiss to the mark.

He closed his eyes, releasing a shuttering breath at the feel of my lips on him. But he didn't push me away. Instead, he ran a light hand along the curve of my face.

Straightening, I traced my fingers over the dozens of additional scars dotting his chest, stopping on the puckered skin on his left bicep.

"And here?"

"We all had numbers tattooed on our arms. When I escaped, one of the first things I did was cut it off. I'd rather have an angry scar than feel like I belonged to anyone."

I pinched my lips together to stop my chin from quivering, every word he spoke making my insides twist and hatred grow. But that wouldn't change what happened to him. Instead, I gave him the only thing I could — my acceptance and understanding.

Leaning closer, I touched another tender kiss to his scar, hoping my gesture would tell him what words alone never could.

"Imogene," he exhaled, his voice barely audible, as if my name simply slipped out unexpectedly.

It was so soft. So gentle.

When he uttered my name in the past, it was more akin to a growl. Not right now.

Right now, the man with me was Samuel.

At least, what was left of him.

"And here?" I peered into his stormy gaze, caressing the angry patch of skin by his collarbone.

"That was the one mark I didn't lie to you about. It *is* a burn mark."

"But it's not from a car accident, is it?"

He slowly shook his head. I wasn't sure what I expected him to tell me, but I never could have prepared myself for the truth.

"Blow torch."

A sob ripped from my throat, and Gideon — Samuel, whoever he was — pulled me against him, comforting me as I struggled to come to terms with the ugly truth of what he endured, all because of the men he once considered friends.

Because of the man *I* considered a friend, too.

All so they could become even richer. Was Samuel's life really worth that much to them?

Pulling my head from his chest, I shifted my attention to the jagged mark running from his ribcage to his hipbone.

"And this?" I ran my finger along the angry blemish.

I sensed I knew exactly what it was from, but I needed to hear it from him.

"I got that when some asshole funeral director patched me up after I was shot by my best friend. But instead of being the good Samaritan I thought he was, the only reason he helped me was so he could sell me for top dollar to a bunch of traffickers, who would make me fight in death matches they broadcast on the dark web."

"I..." I grappled to find the words I needed.

I didn't think any words existed that could convey just how much my heart ached for him. This man had been through hell. Yet he managed to survive. Managed to not give up when it would have been so easy for him to do just that.

Without thinking about the consequences, I grabbed his cheeks and slammed my mouth against his. He stiffened, his hands going to my wrists, as if about to push me away. But he didn't. Not yet.

Instead, we remained in this place, our lips locked in limbo between advance and retreat.

There were a thousand reasons this was a horrible idea.

But there were just as many reasons it may be a good idea, too.

I didn't know. But right now, that didn't matter. I didn't care about the lies. Didn't care about the lives he'd taken. Didn't care that I could lose him all over again. All I did care about was right now.

Having a small taste of Samuel again.

Even if it was the last time.

With a low groan, he moved his hands along my arms and down my back, his touch igniting every nerve with electricity. I melted against him as he pulled me closer, his lips pressed hungrily against mine. He coaxed my mouth open, his tongue swiping against mine in a dance of dominance and surrender that reminded me so damn much of Samuel I couldn't help but release a sob.

He tore away, his concerned eyes scanning me. "What's wrong? Did I hurt you?"

"No." My reply came out as a breathless whisper. I curled my fingers around his nape, forcing his lips back to mine. "You're the only thing that makes it not hurt."

"Imogene," he exhaled before crushing his lips back against mine, stealing my breath and taking it as his own.

And I gave it willingly. I'd give him anything he wanted in order to erase the past. To give him the clean slate he desperately deserved.

"I knew you were a bad idea," he rasped out as he left rough kisses along my jawline, dipping his head into the crook of my neck.

"Why?" I panted.

The feel of his scruff beard and hands roughly exploring my body caused my heartbeat to accelerate, hunger building inside me.

"Because I knew once I had a taste of you again, I'd want more."

His teeth nipped at my skin as he ground his hips against me, his erection hard and thick, even through his shorts.

"That I'd want all of you. That nothing would ever satisfy me again."

"Then have me," I whimpered.

He paused, not moving for several heartbeats as his eyes locked with mine.

Something about the way he peered at me made me think he was about to turn me down. Tell me this wasn't a good idea.

Instead, he slammed his lips against mine, his mouth never breaking from mine as he swooped me into his arms and carried me all the way back into my bedroom.

His bedroom.

"Are you sure about this, Imogene?" he asked once he set me on my feet in front of the bed. "This won't change my plans."

"I don't care about that right now." I pressed my hand to his cheek, and he closed his eyes, melting into my touch. "All I care about is you." I lifted myself onto my toes, brushing a light kiss to the corner of his mouth. "Feeling you." Reaching for the bottom of my t-shirt, I lifted it over my head. "Loving you."

Groaning, he yanked me against him, not even a whisper separating us. Then he crashed his mouth against mine, his tongue tangling with mine as he led me the few feet toward the bed, gently laying me on top of the soft mattress and crawling between my legs.

His hips rocked slow, sensual circles against me as he explored my body with his hands, lowering his mouth toward my exposed breast. My heart raced with anticipation, and I braced to feel his lips on me, his teeth on my nipple. *Something.*

But I never did. Instead, I noticed his attention focus on something other than my breast.

My tattoo.

His Adam's apple bobbed up and down as his fingers traced the familiar pattern, like he once did nearly every day before I'd branded my skin with a permanent reminder of our love.

Dipping his head toward it, he kissed the symbol, his touch so soft and gentle it made me cry.

"Samuel."

His name hung heavy in the room as he slowly lifted

his eyes to mine. It took me several seconds to realize my slip of the tongue.

Once I did, I rushed out, "I'm sorry. Gideon, I—"

He covered my mouth, cutting off my apology with a deep, yet brief kiss.

"Say it again," he pleaded, his lips hovering over mine.

"What?"

"My name. Please, Imogene. Let me hear you say my name again. My *real* name."

The raw need in his voice nearly broke me. I'd do anything to wash away his memories. To remind him of who he was. This man *was* Samuel Tate, regardless of what he believed. I felt it since the beginning. I still felt it now. Those bastards may have tried to take his life. But they didn't take his soul. It was still here. And I'd do everything in my power to bring it back.

"Samuel," I murmured, his name on my lips like a determined prayer. A hopeful benediction. An unwavering promise.

He wrapped his arms around my torso, clinging to me as if I were a life preserver and he was being tossed around a tumultuous ocean.

"Again."

I cradled his face in my hands, forcing his eyes to mine. "Samuel."

"Again."

I inched my mouth toward his. "Your name is Samuel Tate. You were, and still are, the love of my fucking life."

He released a shivering breath, a single tear falling down his cheek as he basked in my words. Then he claimed my mouth, pouring every single emotion he'd experienced over the past five years into the kiss. Fear. Betrayal. Despair. Desolation. Rage. But mixed within all of that was love.

I'd like to think it was this love that helped him survive.

That brought him back to me.

He ran a hand along the contours of my frame, his fingers tracing the delicate tattoo as if no time had passed since the last time he'd done this precise thing. But he didn't linger for too long, straightening as he hooked his fingers into the waistband of my shorts, a single brow arched in question.

But there was no question in my mind. I wanted this. *Needed* this. Needed to feel him again.

"Please, Samuel. Make love to me."

CHAPTER TWENTY-NINE

Gideon

Every voice in my head told me this was a bad idea. That I should walk away. Hell, that I should have walked away the second she started touching my scars.

I'd never been able to keep my head on straight where Imogene was concerned. Her touch, her voice, her very presence made me feel alive. And when she called me Samuel with such tenderness and longing, it felt like coming home after a long journey, stirring something deep inside I thought was dead.

Maybe Henry was right. Maybe Imogene was slowly bringing all the pieces of Samuel out of me once more.

My eyes held hers as I slowly dragged her shorts down her legs, her tattoo stark against her pale skin. I pressed a tender kiss to the symbol of her unconditional love, then stood, pushing my own shorts down, her gaze burning into me, full of greed as she stared at my erection.

I loved how much she craved me. Loved how her body responded to me. Loved how free she was with me.

Giving my cock a few more strokes, I returned to her and captured her mouth in a heated kiss. Hunger and desperation mingled together as I circled my hips, teasing her clit with my throbbing erection. She released a tiny moan, her breaths coming shorter and faster as desire coursed through her body.

"Please, Samuel," she begged, digging her nails into my back.

I winced slightly. My back may have been mostly scar tissue at this point, but I still had several spots that were more sensitive to touch than others, especially along my spine.

When she noticed my expression, she immediately dropped her hold on me. "Did I hurt you? Your scars. I—"

I silenced her concerns with a kiss, tugging on her bottom lip. "Do it again."

"Are you sure? I don't want to cause you pain."

"I said..." I slowly rocked my hips against her, hitting that little bundle of nerves once more. "Do. It. Again." I hovered my lips over hers, bringing my hand to her throat and squeezing lightly. "I thought you knew how satisfying a little pain with your pleasure could be."

"I certainly do," she said with a smirk as she dug her nails harder into my skin. I rewarded her by tightening my grip on her neck, rubbing my erection against her clit, praying I didn't lose it before I could bury myself inside of her.

But I needed this more.

Or maybe Imogene did.

"Again," I urged her.

And again, she dragged her nails down my back, and I roared through the mixture of pain and pleasure. With every ounce of pressure I added to her throat, she rubbed her slick cunt harder against me, burrowing her nails deeper into my flesh. I didn't know how much longer I could last, the sensation of pleasure and pain almost unbearable.

Finally, she spasmed around me, her muscles clenching and convulsing in a frenzy of ecstasy. I quickly removed my hands from their tight grip on her throat, and she sucked in a welcome gulp of air. I covered her mouth, giving her my breath as I eased inside her, relishing in the warmth that enveloped me as we became one, moving in perfect harmony.

I resisted the urge to go hard and fast, wanting to remember every shiver, every circle, every moan. Instead, I kissed her slow and deep as I made love to her the way I once did, savoring the moment as if this was the last time I'd ever feel her.

She very well could change her mind about us tomorrow morning. She *should* change her mind about us tomorrow morning.

I wasn't lying when I told her I wasn't a good person. It was probably the one honest thing I *had* told her. I had more blood on my hands than even her sorry excuse of a father. I'd taken countless lives, some because it was the only way I'd live. Others because they hurt Imogene. Others because they hurt me.

It was only a matter of time before my bad deeds caught up to me.

But right now, as my body trembled with more pleasure than I thought possible, none of that mattered, Imogene's touch erasing any doubt or guilt from my mind.

It had only been mere days since we'd done this, but tonight felt different. Even when I showed her my scars that first time, it didn't compare to this level of intimacy.

Because now, there were no more lies caught between us. We were finally free to be who we were always meant to be. The people I never thought we'd be again.

At least the person I never thought *I'd* be again.

Maybe I was wrong.

Could we find our way back to the people we once were?

I'd given up hope of that ever happening, a slave to my revenge.

Yet, with every thrust and kiss, Imogene seemed to chip away at my compulsion, making me think there could be more to life than just darkness and pain.

More than revenge.

"Please, Samuel," she moaned, wrapping her legs tighter around my waist, urging me to increase my rhythm, her skin slick with sweat. "Faster."

I shook my head, sliding my hands up her arms and intertwining my fingers with hers, pinning them to the pillow.

"Like this, Imogene." I moved in a deliciously slow circle, her back arching as I hit the spot that drove her crazy. "I don't want to rush this. Want you to feel me. Not Gideon. But Samuel."

Tonight wasn't just about satisfying our carnal urges, as was the case when she thought I was Gideon Saint. Instead, tonight was about reminding each other who we once were before all the pain and betrayal destroyed everything.

"I do feel you. I always have. Even after that first time we were together, I knew it was you," she confessed. "Only one man has ever made me feel the things you did." She craned toward me, chasing after my kiss. "The things you do."

My lips collided with hers as we poured all the emotions we'd locked up for years into the kiss. I couldn't even be upset that she figured out the truth of who I was from the beginning. It was a testament to the connection we once shared. And as I moved inside of her with increasing desperation, I was convinced that hadn't changed, even with the passing of time.

If anything, it felt even stronger now, considering everything we'd been through.

Shouldn't that have been enough?

I wanted it to be, but at what cost?

Could I really let Liam and James get away with all the pain they'd caused? Could I risk allowing them to be free to hurt even more people?

But when I felt Imogene's muscles clench around me, I pushed the thought away, focusing on the incredible woman in my arms.

"Samuel," she moaned again, her breaths ragged and desperate as she gripped my hands with a bruising force. Each gasp from her lips ignited a fire in my veins, pushing me closer to the edge of oblivion.

"Yeah, baby." I nuzzled into the shallow of her neck, nipping my teeth against her sensitive skin.

"I'm about to—"

"Do it," I ordered. "Let go."

I released her hands, tracing my fingers along her torso until they found her soaked clit, rubbing it as I thrust harder. That was all it took for her to detonate, her body convulsing as wave after wave of bliss rolled through her.

"Damn, you are so fucking beautiful when you come, Imogene," I grunted, picking up the pace in the hopes of prolonging her orgasm. "I don't know if I can hold on much longer."

She ran her hands down my back. "Let me feel you."

"Do you want me to—"

"All of you," she interrupted, answering the question on my mind.

I was about to ask if she was sure when she grabbed my ass, only allowing me enough room to continue my rhythm.

"Please, Samuel." She curved toward me, taking my earlobe between her teeth. "Come inside of me."

Hearing those words was all I needed, and I let go of what little restraint I had left, giving in completely to the primal urge coursing through me.

When I had nothing left, I collapsed on top of her, the only sound our labored breathing and hearts racing in time with each other. I adjusted our bodies so she lay beside me, her back to my front.

Then I did the one thing I never thought I'd do again. I fell asleep with Imogene in my arms as I traced the symbol of unconditional love on her hip.

CHAPTER THIRTY

Imogene

The ocean churned beneath me as I bobbed up and down on my surfboard, the darkness of the predawn hours surrounding me like a cocoon. After last night, I needed to come out here. Needed to think. Needed to figure out what to do about Gideon—Samuel.

He'd killed Alton.

And he planned to kill James and Liam, too.

What they did to him was horrible, but could I just stay quiet, knowing what he planned to do? Wouldn't that make me just as culpable?

I'd struggled with this same thing when my sperm donor kidnapped me. For three horrific days, I was forced to watch him brutally torture and kill several women.

And I did nothing to stop him, too paralyzed by fear and trauma.

The guilt over that plagued me for years.

Hell, it *still* plagued me.

Could I stand having even more blood on my hands?

I'd hoped coming out here before the sun rose would offer me some sort of clarity. It didn't.

Especially since Gideon currently sat watch from his usual spot at The Daily Grind.

It was the only way he'd let me surf this morning, too concerned about what Liam might do.

It was endearing, yet suffocating at the same time. How could I find clarity when the source of my confusion watched my every move?

I shifted my gaze from the shore, peering toward the horizon and watching the swells as I waited for a wave. Finally, I saw one in the distance heading for me, the timing perfect.

As it approached, I readied myself, studying the wave with every inch it erased before paddling hard and hopping up on my board.

The water was rougher this morning than it had been earlier in the week, the ocean more unpredictable. But I held on, concentrating only on the wave.

Until something below the surface caught my attention.

It looked like a hand.

I tried to maintain my balance, but I was too distracted. The wave engulfed me, dragging me down to the ocean's depths. In the darkness, I was disoriented, unsure which way was up. Trying to remain calm, I looked for the bubbles and followed them to the surface, fighting against the rough water to swim to shore.

Coughing and gasping for air, I managed to stumble to the sand and collapse on my knees. It took several minutes for me to catch my breath. Once I did, a renewed wave of panic overtook me when I noticed my hands were covered in blood. I frantically scanned my body for the source, but there were no cuts. No scratches. No marks.

Instead, as I surveyed the shoreline, I found it was littered with bodies, the ocean painted red.

And on the very top of the pile was Alton Sinclair, his lifeless eyes staring at me in accusation.

My screams echoed against the vast emptiness, but no one seemed to hear me, even when I was pulled back under the sea of blood.

The last thing I remembered was the smirk on Gideon's face as I took my final breath.

My eyes snapped open, sweat drenching my body, my hands shaking uncontrollably. I pressed a hand to my chest, trying to slow my racing heart as each detail of my dream continued to haunt me in vivid clarity. The blood-red ocean waves crashing around me, drowning out my screams felt so real, to the point that I couldn't help but question whether it had been merely a nightmare or something more sinister. A warning of what was to come.

I took several deep breaths, trying to calm myself and push away the unsettled feeling that clung to me like a relentless predator.

Between the dream and waking up to find Samuel's side of the bed empty, I was more confused than ever, my head at war with my heart.

Would I have felt better if he were still here, his arms wrapped around me?

I couldn't say with certainty.

These days, I couldn't say *anything* with certainty.

Carefully getting to my feet, I headed across the room and into the bathroom. The hot water from the shower felt like heaven on my sore body, washing away my doubt and anxiety for a moment. Then I pulled on a fresh pair of shorts and a t-shirt before going in search of Samuel.

But when I entered the living room and kitchen, I found it devoid of life. Maybe he went with Henry to oversee the installation of the new security system at my townhouse.

I started to head back upstairs to grab my phone and

text him when a couple of voices caught my attention. My curiosity getting the better of me, I tiptoed toward a partially open door at the end of the hallway.

"What a tragedy. Missing without a trace."

I paused at the amusement in Samuel's tone. But there was something else, too. Something dark and sinister.

It was completely out of character for the man I once knew.

For Samuel.

Because this *wasn't* Samuel. Despite the connection I thought we shared last night, he was back to being Gideon Saint.

Back to carrying out his plan for revenge.

"It's not just making headlines in Atlanta, but across the country now," Henry stated.

"Can you turn it up?"

A female voice filled the room from what I assumed to be a news broadcast. "The police still have no leads on the whereabouts of Brian McGuire, a respected funeral director here in Atlanta. He failed to show up for work on Monday. The last known communication from him was on Sunday afternoon. The police urge anyone with information to reach out."

I flashed back to everything Gideon shared with me, including the name of the funeral director who patched him up and sold him.

Brian McGuire.

Now, that same man hadn't been seen or heard from since Sunday.

The same day Gideon approached me at the bar.

Was *this* the reason he was in Atlanta?

My stomach churned the more I thought about that night.

As I did, one thing in particular stood out in my mind — pushing off his suit jacket and finding blood on it.

I thought he'd hurt himself.

Was it this man's blood I'd found? How much time had passed between when he killed a man and when he fucked me? An hour? Less?

"What's the plan? Want to move on James right away?" Henry asked, cutting through my unease.

As much as I wanted to find the nearest bathroom and expel whatever contents were left in my stomach, I was rooted to the spot, unable to put one foot in front of the other.

"Let them sweat for a few more days," Gideon stated, his voice calculated and cold. "As of right now, Liam still has no idea what James did. He's freaking out over Imogene's line of questioning while James is panicking over what the police will uncover once they go through Brian's files. It'll probably take them a little longer to learn James was the last person to see him alive. We'll wait until then to send the recording to every major news outlet in the country."

"Not the police?"

"The court of public opinion can do infinitely more damage. Plus, this will force the police to take action instead of accepting a bribe to keep quiet about his involvement."

"And that's what you want? For the police to get involved?"

There was a pause, and I held my breath, waiting for his answer. A part of me prayed he'd answer in the affirmative. Prayed he still had some decency left.

"I do."

"Why? You didn't want the police involved in Alton's downfall. You insisted on taking care of him yourself."

"Because Alton's crimes weren't that bad. Sure, he was a prick who stole people's life savings, but James... He's the reason Jonah was beaten so badly in prison that he turned into a vegetable. I want James to suffer the same fate. After all, he's a former prosecutor. Pretty sure some of the people he put away would love to get their hands on him."

"Releasing the audio recording will most likely reopen the investigation into your death," Henry remarked gravely. "It might spook Liam, even if it doesn't mention him specifically. It'll be proof that James conspired with *someone* to kill you."

"Which is why we'll need to move on Liam right away."

"Will you be ready?"

"Trust me. I've been waiting to torture that mother fucker since the day I escaped," Gideon replied harshly. "It's time he finally understands the true price of his greed."

The more I listened, the sicker I felt.

Part of me understood his need for revenge. But another part recoiled at hearing him talk so callously about taking a life, as if it was of little consequence to him. It reminded me too much of my sperm donor.

I whirled around, wanting to get out of this place, to hell with whether Gideon thought it was safe for me to return to my townhouse. It was safer than being in such close quarters as someone who willingly admitted to killing another man.

And who planned to do it again.

But as I attempted to retreat without alerting anyone to my presence, my feet made more noise against the hardwood floor than I'd intended, and the door flew open.

"Imogene."

I didn't stop. Instead, I kept my head down, wishing I'd soon wake up from this nightmare.

But I wouldn't.

I'd gone through the same thing in the days following Samuel's death. Back then, I would have given anything to have Samuel back, but not like this. Because the Samuel I knew wouldn't be so casual about taking another man's life.

And *that* was the Samuel I wanted to remember.

Not this...stranger.

"Imogene, wait!" Gideon thundered, wrapping his hand around my wrist and yanking me to a stop.

"Don't touch me," I demanded.

He immediately released me, confusion swirling in his blue eyes.

The same blue eyes I peered into last night as he made love to me. Now they were different. Cold and hardened, reflecting the callousness of his tormented soul.

"What's wrong?" He stepped closer, but didn't make a move to touch me.

I squeezed my eyes shut, trying to get my thoughts in order. "I just..." I lifted my gaze to his. "I don't know if I can do this."

"Do what?"

"This." I gestured between our bodies. "Whatever this is. Last night, I saw the old Samuel again. And a part of me thought that maybe I could bring you back. That I could fix you. Or save you. I don't know what exactly.

But now?" I shook my head. "After hearing everything I just did, I don't recognize this person who's actively planning another man's murder."

His jaw clenched, and I could hear his argument without him uttering a word.

Because it was the same argument I'd had with myself over the past several days.

"I get it," I continued before he could say anything in his defense. "I understand these bastards betrayed you. That you had to endure things…"

I trailed off, my voice catching as my emotions overwhelmed me from the memory of his scars. Tracing my fingers along them last night. Kissing each one, hoping it would be enough for him to move on from his past.

How foolish of me to have thought that.

"The other day when I overheard your conversation with Henry, something you said stood out to me."

"What's that?"

"That you wanted to keep the truth from me because you didn't want me to know what you've become."

His Adam's apple bobbed up and down in a hard swallow as vulnerability flickered over his features.

Despite the perfectly tailored suit he wore, I saw a glimpse of the old Samuel again, the man who was so full of love and compassion I couldn't help but give him my heart. But I knew how this would go. I'd been here countless times over the past few weeks, even if I didn't realize it at the time. In a matter of minutes, Samuel would disappear and Gideon would take his place.

How much longer until Gideon eliminated what was left of Samuel, just like he eliminated Alton and Brian McGuire? How he planned to soon eliminate James and Liam?

"I'm begging you to leave me alone. Let me hold on to the good memories I have of Samuel. No more mornings at the coffee shop. No more keeping tabs on me. Just...let me forget I ever heard the name Gideon Saint." My voice caught at the thought, but I had to do this for my own wellbeing. "Let me remember Samuel Tate the way he deserves to be remembered. For all the good he once did. Not the...monster he's become."

Tears threatened to spill over, but I kept them at bay, not wanting to give him a reason to comfort me. Not wanting to fall under his spell again. My heart couldn't take much more of this tumultuous tug-of-war it had fallen victim to since the day I first noticed the man with familiar blue eyes.

"After everything you've put me through, I deserve that much," I choked out.

He parted his lips, his gaze holding me captive for what felt like an eternity, my plea hanging heavy in the air between us. I sensed he wanted to say something. To argue. To tell me he'd stop this desperate need for revenge and close this chapter of his life.

Or maybe that was what *I* wanted him to say.

"You deserve to move on," he said very matter-of-factly.

"You do, too."

"I don't think I can," he admitted, his eyes searching mine for understanding. "Not until I finish this. Not until I know none of them are a threat."

"Then this needs to be goodbye," I managed to squeak out, the sharp stab of pain in my throat making it difficult to speak.

He sighed deeply, but didn't protest or try to convince me otherwise.

Instead, he clutched my cheeks, causing me to suck in a quick intake of air as electricity heated my veins from his familiar touch. Regardless of his actions, I couldn't find the strength to push away. I stared into the blue eyes that were once filled with so much love, but were now clouded with lies and deception.

With agonizing slowness, he leaned down and pressed a soft kiss to my lips, lingering for several heartbreaking seconds as I breathed him in for the last time. He held me close and, for a moment, I almost expected for him to change his mind. To sweep me into his arms and promise me I was enough. That I was more important than this need for revenge.

But he didn't, releasing his hold on me and stepping back.

"Henry will drive you home."

He didn't even meet my eyes. Instead, he simply turned and retreated down the hallway without a single look back.

I thought losing Samuel all those years ago was the hardest thing I ever had to do.

But this? Knowing the man I once loved was alive, yet I still pushed him away regardless? It destroyed me. What did he expect, though? That I'd be okay with his plan for revenge?

I already had to bury Samuel once.

I couldn't do it again.

Instead, I needed to keep him alive in the only place he was safe...

My memories.

CHAPTER THIRTY-ONE

Gideon

"Are you sure about this?" Henry asked as I peered at my reflection in the mirror of my suite at the Beverly Hills hotel where a political fundraiser was being held.

Normally, I hated everything to do with politics, but I was willing to make an exception today, considering Senator James Turner was also on the guest list.

And I couldn't wait to see the look on his face when he realized exactly who was responsible for the missing funeral director.

James had been unraveling all week. Not just because he worried the police may soon learn he hired Brian McGuire to dispose of a body years ago. But also because he feared Liam would find out he never *did* dispose of that body, even after he'd assured him it was all taken care of.

As if Brian McGuire's disappearance wasn't stressful enough for poor James, an anonymous tip to the Atlanta police linked him directly to the funeral home on the day Brian was last seen.

James claimed he was simply planning Alton Sinclair's memorial, but the detective assigned to the case didn't seem so convinced, regardless of James' insistence he had nothing to do with Brian's disappearance.

For once, he was telling the truth.

It wouldn't do him any good, though.

"Of course I'm sure," I responded, adjusting my bowtie.

I hated wearing these damn things, but it was necessary for the part I needed to play as a billionaire business owner and philanthropist.

"Like I told you from the beginning..." I met Henry's gaze in the mirror. "These bastards deserve to know what it's like to have everything they love taken from them." I turned to face him. "By the end of tonight, James Turner will know exactly what that feels like."

"I'm just making sure you haven't had any second thoughts."

He didn't come right out and say it, but I knew he wasn't merely referring to how I planned to go about disposing of James.

Instead, he was asking if I'd had any second thoughts about Imogene.

The reminder of her made my heart ache, a sharp pain that threatened to consume me. But after everything I put her through, the least I could do was let her hold on to her good memories of Samuel.

And over the past week, that was precisely what I did.

I stopped going to The Daily Grind in the morning. Stopped driving by her house. Stopped sneaking into the owner's box at the soccer stadium to check on her during practice or games.

After watching her every day for the better part of the past year, it had been difficult to quit her cold turkey.

But I wasn't willing to give up my plan for revenge.

So I gave up Imogene instead.

I kept waiting for my house to be swarmed with law enforcement, considering everything she knew. But that never happened.

Even though I broke her heart, she still kept my secret. She was still loyal.

And how did I return that loyalty?

By continuing down the same destructive path I set out on months ago.

"An eye for an eye, Henry," I reminded him, my tone hard and determined. "We agreed. Once that first domino fell, there was no going back. I already have too much blood on my hands. May as well make it count. Make sure it hasn't all been for nothing."

He closed his eyes, blowing out a long breath, his disagreement clear. But he'd never abandon me. After all the shit we went through in that foster home, we swore to always have each other's back, no matter what.

"Brothers in blood," he said with a sigh, reciting the same oath we often did during our worst moments.

I hooked my pinky finger with his. "Brothers in blood," I repeated, holding his gaze.

"You should get going," Henry said, stepping away. "We're on a schedule tonight."

"Right. Of course." I did one last check of my appearance, then headed toward the door.

"Just a reminder, you may be flying blind in there." Henry followed me into the living room, his faded Nirvana t-shirt and cargo shorts at odds with the tuxedo I wore.

I'd give anything to trade places with him, but this was the choice I'd made. In order to destroy these men, I had to become one of them.

"With the president being in attendance, secret service will be swarming the place. As much as I love you, I'd rather not go to prison for hacking into their security system."

"I'll be fine," I promised with a squeeze to his bicep. "I've got it all under control."

"I hope so."

I gave him one last reassuring look, then slipped out of the suite.

As I entered the gleaming ballroom after a thorough pat down, courtesy of the secret service, I was greeted by swarms of people arriving for tonight's event. Men in tailored tuxedos and women adorned in designer gowns flooded the space, laughing and smiling as if they didn't have a care in the world.

My skin crawled from all the fake people surrounding me. Celebrities. Politicians. Business moguls. Anyone willing to cough up nearly a half-million dollars for the privilege of attending this exclusive event.

And this was a truth I had to face when I saw my best friend point a gun at me.

Some people would do anything to have a seat at the table.

I may not have known any of these people personally, but I knew their type — driven by money and power, sharks willing to tear each other apart. They didn't care who they had to hurt on their way up the ladder as long as they made it to the top. And these people had a great view from up this high.

But they were all too blinded by their lust for success to realize that the higher they climbed, the farther they'd fall.

And James Turner was about to plummet... After I gave him a little push.

In between sips of champagne from a passing server's tray, I headed deeper into the room, scanning the hundreds of people for one in particular. The smooth sounds of jazz music filled the air as I weaved through conversations and polite greetings from acquaintances who recognized me from Liam's recent charity golf tournament. But I had no interest in making small talk tonight.

Thankfully, it didn't take me much longer to find the reason I'd spent a fortune on a ticket to tonight's event. Sure, I could have confronted James in his office. Maybe even at his overpriced mansion in Brentwood.

But I liked the idea of doing it here. In a place where he felt comfortable and untouchable.

After politely excusing myself from a conversation with the head of a pharmaceutical company who hoped to increase his profits in the next quarter by raising prices of medication even more, I made my way toward the bar, studying James as he scrolled through his phone while waiting for the bartender to finish pouring scotch into a glass.

He looked put together, his tuxedo crisp and shoes polished, but I didn't miss the way he constantly surveyed his surroundings, as if waiting for the police to storm in and arrest him at any moment.

That didn't keep him away from tonight's gala, though. Like Liam, he'd never miss an opportunity to hobnob amongst people who might help him climb the next rung of the ladder, even if he'd eventually step on them on his way up.

"Senator Turner," I said brightly as I approached.

He stilled, his eyes widening in surprise. It was obvious he didn't expect to see me here. Being the politician he was, he recovered quickly, extending his hand toward me with a practiced smile, regardless of the things Liam may have said about me in his presence.

"Mr. Saint. What a pleasant surprise. I didn't realize you were a big donor to President Campbell's campaign."

"I donate to both parties." I shook his hand, then took another sip from my champagne as James all but downed his scotch, signaling the bartender for another. "In my line of work, I've found it pays to back both horses, so to speak. That way, I'm bound to walk away with something I want."

"Right." He threw a handful of bills on the counter, swiping his fresh scotch and taking another large swallow.

"I heard the news," I announced as he was about to leave.

"The news?" His face paled, and he anxiously licked his lips, glancing over his shoulder. "I'm not sure—"

"About Alton Sinclair."

He pushed out a breath, visibly relieved. "Right. Of course."

"I'm very sorry for your loss," I offered in mock sincerity.

"Thank you."

"It's curious though, isn't it?" I asked casually.

"What is?" He scrunched his brows.

"Your friend dies, then a few days later, you're the last one to see that funeral director in Atlanta alive."

His mouth agape, he blinked repeatedly. "How..." He paused, swallowing hard. "How do you know about that?"

"I make it my business to know everything about everyone. Just like I know all about the conversation you had with Brian McGuire before he...disappeared."

"He's planning Alton's service. Now if you'll excuse me."

He attempted to brush past me, but I stepped in front of him, hooking my arm around his shoulders in a friendly manner, as if we were two old friends reconnecting after a long time apart.

Bringing my phone to his ear, I hit play, watching his complexion blanch as he listened to his last conversation with Brian McGuire where he admitted to selling me. To make matters worse, both men had addressed the other by their name, leaving no question as to who was speaking.

"Is that really the story you want to go with?" I asked nonchalantly after a minute, dropping my hold on him.

He made no move to escape, too stunned to put one foot in front of the other.

"Imagine what this could do to your career if the police got a hold of it." My eyes widened in fake shock. "Or worse, the media."

"How did you get that?" he seethed.

"How I got it isn't important. All that matters is I have it."

He didn't say anything for several moments, but I could sense the wheels spinning in his head as he tried to wrap his mind around what this could mean for him and his career.

"How much do you want?" he finally demanded, his question dripping with disdain.

I let out a low chuckle before lifting my champagne flute to my lips. The bubbles danced on my tongue as I savored the taste of victory.

"It's so typical for you to think I'm after your money."

"What other reason is there?"

Leaning closer, I made sure he could see the fire in my eyes as I spoke my response with calculated precision.

"Vengeance."

My voice was barely above a whisper, but it echoed around us like a booming clap of thunder, drowning out the polite chatter of the wealthy elite.

"For years, I've dreamed of this moment," I continued. "At first, I was only after you because of what you did to Jonah."

The instant that name left my mouth, all the remaining color drained from his face. Beads of sweat dotted his brow and his hands trembled ever so slightly.

"Jonah," he repeated, his voice hoarse with fear and confusion. "What are you—"

"But after hearing that little conversation, I'm doing it for me, too."

"Doing what?" he asked, frozen in place.

"What you deserve," I hissed, keeping my tone deathly calm, as if we were discussing the weather. Not his eventual downfall. "I'm going to watch you lose everything you care about. Money. Power. Influence. By this time tomorrow, you'll be yet another in a long line of disgraced politicians. Then you'll know exactly how I felt when I woke up in the hell your greed sent me to."

"My greed? I don't— Who are you?"

"Curious about finding Samuel Tate's fingerprints on that glass in Alton's cabin. Isn't it?"

James shook his head. "How did you..."

When I lifted my champagne glass back to my lips

with a smirk, he trailed off, his expression widening in realization.

"Thanks for the chat, old friend." I patted his back somewhat harshly, causing him to cough. "I do hope you'll enjoy the rest of your evening. I know I'll enjoy mine." I downed the rest of my champagne, then left him alone at the bar.

It was official. This was the best half-million dollars I'd ever spent.

CHAPTER THIRTY-TWO

Imogene

"You really don't mind staying in tonight?" I asked Melanie as she plopped beside me on her couch, both of us wearing pajamas, even though it was only seven in the evening.

After this past week, I had no desire to get dressed up and go out to some obnoxiously loud club in Hollywood.

"Of course not." She handed me an overflowing glass of wine.

I took a tiny sip and placed it on the coffee table. I didn't feel like drinking. I hadn't felt like much of anything this week.

"At least here I don't have to wait in line for a drink and the bartender always has a generous pour." She smirked, taking a large gulp from her own wine before facing me.

"So tell me... How are things? Despite the obvious with Ollie," she added quickly with a compassionate smile. "How's Gideon?"

Just hearing that name sent a sharp pang through my chest. I couldn't deny that I missed him, but did I miss Gideon? Or Samuel?

"Uh oh."

I snapped my eyes toward her. "What?"

"Do I sense trouble in hot-sex paradise? Please tell me you didn't let the whole fingerprint thing interfere with Gideon," she added, reaching for my hand and squeezing. "Learning Sam's fingerprints were found at Alton's cabin must have been a shock, but he's gone. He—"

"He *is* Sam," I blurted out before I could stop myself.

She dropped her hold on me. "Ginny, you heard what all the investigators said."

I dug my fingers through my hair, messing it up even more. "Trust me, Mel. I was just as surprised as you are. I convinced myself I was losing my mind. But it turns out I was right all along. Gideon Saint *is* Samuel Tate. He admitted it. Along with a lot of other stuff."

Silence permeated the room as Melanie stared at me, her jaw agape, barely even blinking for several long moments. I could sense her wanting to chastise me for overreacting once more. But the longer she looked into my eyes, the more she must have realized I wasn't over-reacting.

Even though I wished I were.

"Sam's alive?" she squeaked out, her shock palpable.

I knew all too well how she felt. I went through the same thing myself.

"Where has he been all this time?"

"A place worse than hell," I responded through the heaviness in my throat.

She shook her head, her eyes clouded with tears. "I don't—"

"I'll tell you everything, but it needs to stay between us."

I doubted she'd go to Liam or anyone else with the truth, considering she repeatedly insisted my relation-ship with him was toxic, something I now fully agreed with. But I couldn't stomach the idea of anything happening to her because she said something she shouldn't.

"No one else can know what I'm about to tell you." I held her gaze so she could see the importance of this. "Not even your father."

Although, based on the way he questioned Gideon during the golf tournament, he must have sensed some-thing was amiss. But I doubt he could have predicted this.

"I promise, Gin. Your secrets are safe with me." She swallowed hard. "So are Sam's. You can trust me."

I took a deep breath, then began to unravel the web of secrets I had no choice but to come to terms with over the past few weeks.

How, five years ago, Liam shot him when he refused to sell their company to ImageScape.

How a man named Brian McGuire was hired to take care of the crime scene and leave only enough evidence so Jonah would appear at fault, but when he arrived, Samuel was still alive.

How Brian and James conspired to sell him to a human trafficker in order to make money, still staging the crime scene to make it look like Jonah had shot and killed him to cover their tracks.

How Samuel spent nearly four years fighting for his life in underground death matches broadcast on the dark web.

How, one night, he escaped when the van he was in crashed.

How he found a cabin by a lake where he could get cleaned up and figure out what to do next.

How he called me, but I hung up on him, thinking he was someone trying to play a cruel joke on me.

How he made his way to Atlanta so I could see with my own eyes it was him, even if his face had been beaten and disfigured.

How he saw me with Liam and felt betrayed, considering the role he'd played.

How he went to Henry, who took him in and nursed him back to health.

How all the injuries he suffered required him to endure extensive surgery.

How he decided to change his appearance since he was having facial reconstructive surgery.

How the scars covering his body weren't from a car accident but were the result of all the torture he endured for years.

How he vowed to make those who betrayed him suffer as he did.

Then I told her how I learned he was Samuel in the first place.

How I noticed similar burns when I was looking at pictures of Samuel the night I learned about his fingerprints being found.

How I accused Gideon of being Samuel after confirming he had marks in the same location.

How he then accused me of only wanting to be with him because he reminded me of Samuel.

How I went to Atlanta to clear my mind.

How Gideon was also there and we both apologized for our behavior.

How, when I left his hotel suite the following morning, I ran into Henry Fontaine getting off the elevator.

How I saw him approach Gideon's door.

How I followed him, if for no other reason than to dispel my suspicions.

Then how I overheard Gideon admit he *was* Samuel Tate, confirming what I'd known in my heart all along.

"This is…" Melanie shook her head, searching for the right words to communicate everything she was thinking and feeling after listening to the story I'd kept from her for the past week.

"A lot. I get it. I struggled to believe it all myself. It seemed so far-fetched."

She snapped her gaze back to mine. "Oh, I definitely believe his story."

I furrowed my brow. "You do?"

"Don't you?"

"I do now. At first, I was skeptical. I *wanted* to believe him, but it was hard after all the lies. So he told me that the next time I saw Liam to mention a detective had reached out to ask me about Samuel Tate's death."

"Did you?"

I nodded.

"And Liam?"

"The second I mentioned it and Liam's face went pale, I knew he was telling the truth. Knew Liam had…" I trailed off, my throat closing up over how blind I'd been. How easily I'd allowed Liam to manipulate me.

Melanie gave my hand another reassuring squeeze. It

didn't escape my notice that she didn't seem all too surprised to learn this about Liam.

"Karma will make him pay."

I didn't have it in me to correct her, remind her it was Gideon — not karma — who would make him pay.

"So where does this leave the two of you?" she asked, taking a small sip of her wine. "After I hunt him down and give him a piece of my mind for lying, of course."

Normally, I would have found some humor in her words, but right now, I couldn't even muster a fake laugh.

"There can't be an us. I thought there could be, but this man he's become... He's not the Samuel Tate I fell in love with."

A long pause settled in her apartment as she digested my words, the only sound the distant hum of traffic from the street below. Then she turned her attention back to me, her brows furrowed and lips pursed.

"Let me see if I have this straight," she clipped out. "You learn that Samuel Tate is alive after years of wishing he were and you're just going to...walk away?"

"He's *not* Samuel," I insisted. "He may have the same DNA, but he's not the same person."

"But you knew it was him, Gin. Almost from the beginning."

"What does that have to do with anything?" I lowered my voice. "He killed Alton. And that missing funeral director in Atlanta? He was the cleaner James conspired with to sell Samuel. Considering he went missing the same time Gideon just so happened to be in Atlanta, it's all but a certainty he killed him, too. And I know he also plans on making sure James and Liam die, too."

"You never would have even considered he was Sam if you didn't see pieces of him, despite his changed appearance. Would you?"

I parted my lips to argue, but she cut me off once more.

"When you learned he'd been shot and was presumed dead, you would have given anything to have Sam back. Right?"

"You know I would have, but—"

"Well, he's back. He might not be the same, but neither are you, Gin. You've changed since then, too. *Everyone* has. Everyone changes. That's part of life. No one stays the same forever. Don't throw this away because you're stuck in the past."

"I'm not stuck in the past." I jumped to my feet. "If anything, *he's* the one stuck in the past. He's killing people, Melanie. How can you expect me to be okay with that?"

She met my gaze, her expression calm and measured, at odds with the turmoil swirling inside me. "There is no black and white, only varying shades of gray."

"What does that even mean?" I placed my hands on my hips.

"It's something my aunt says," she explained, standing and walking toward me, running her hands down my arms. "You like to look at the world in absolutes — black and white. Good and bad. Right and wrong. But life doesn't work that way. Some people do good things for bad reasons. And others do bad things for good reasons."

Her words reminded me of what Gideon told me when he finally confessed his truth.

"And you think he has a good reason for this?" I shot back incredulously. "For playing God, more or less."

"I can understand it."

I shook my head, although I shouldn't have been surprised by her response. After all, her argument sounded a hell of a lot like the one I'd been having with myself all week.

"He still lied to me," I stammered out. "How can a relationship possibly work after such a huge betrayal?"

"He had his reasons for lying."

"Yeah." I crossed my arms in front of my chest. "To get into my pants."

She opened and closed her mouth several times, probably trying to find the best words to tell me I was being irrational.

But I wasn't.

I was hurt.

Confused.

And a myriad of other emotions I couldn't even begin to make sense of.

"Did I ever tell you my parents' story?" she finally asked, moving back to the couch and sitting down.

I joined her. "No."

"They knew each other when they were kids," she began. "But when my mom was six, she and her parents were in a car accident. My dad thought she'd died. Turns out, my grandfather purposefully hid her away. So when she and my dad crossed paths again as adults and he realized she was the same girl he thought was dead, he was shocked. Even so, he hid the truth about who they were to each other."

"Why?"

"To protect her," Melanie explained. "He figured his father must have had a damn good reason to hide her away and tell him she was dead. And I think the same could be said for Sam. He has a lot of reasons he didn't want to tell you the truth, some more selfish than others. But I also believe your safety has always been his top priority. Hell, the man snapped some fucker's neck to save your life. You may think that the man you've been spending time with is nothing like the old Sam, but he's still a good person, even if he is a bit...morally gray." She paused, narrowing her gaze on me. "He's not like your sperm donor."

"But he's taken lives," I said softly, renewing my argument. Clinging to it like it was the last lifeboat on the Titanic.

"You knew that before you ever slept with him. You *saw* him kill a man with his bare hands."

"That was different," I argued, albeit rather unconvincingly.

"Are you upset because he's done bad things?" She gave me a knowing look. "Or because it *doesn't* bother you like you wish it did?"

I blinked, my response on the tip of my tongue, but the words wouldn't come. Not when she'd seen past the carefully constructed façade to the true fear that caused me to push away the one man who'd always owned my heart.

I'd claimed I understood why Samuel was doing this, even if I'd never choose this path. The only reason I struggled with it was because of my biological father. He took lives without remorse and, because of that, he was a bad person.

Samuel took lives, too.

But did that *truly* make him a bad person?

As much as I wanted to condemn him for his choices, I couldn't ignore the fact that my mother had taken a life, as well. She'd killed my sperm donor. And not in self-defense, like I'd originally believed.

Instead, my mother knew she'd never be free if she didn't put an end to him. So she took matters into her own hands. Got herself the justice she and so many of his other victims deserved.

Wasn't that all Samuel was doing now? Getting himself the justice he desperately deserved?

If I was going to fault him for his actions, I'd be a hypocrite if I didn't find my mother equally guilty.

"He may not look like Samuel anymore, but his heart, his soul…" Melanie clutched my hand in hers. "That's still Samuel. Maybe it's a little darker than it used to be, but there's a little darkness in all of us. Are you really willing to lose him all over again?"

"I…" I squeezed my eyes shut, my thoughts a jumbled mess.

Flashes of memories flooded my mind — moments when it was just us. When he didn't have to pretend to be someone else in front of Liam or James or even Melanie.

In those quiet moments, he *was* Samuel, despite his insistence that Samuel was dead.

Maybe he just needed me to show him he was still in there. Show him the things he endured hadn't destroyed him.

I jumped to my feet, my mind spinning. "I'm sorry. I—"

"No apologies necessary." She waved me off as she stood. "Go get your man. And when you're done screwing his brains out, tell him he owes me a visit. And some of that smoked brisket he used to make. I'll forgive all his bullshit for some of that."

"Duly noted," I said as she enveloped me in a hug before I rushed into the guest bedroom and threw all my things into my bag.

As I drove away from Melanie's apartment, I tuned out the constant buzz of sirens and helicopters circling overhead. Instead, all my thoughts were of getting to Samuel as quickly as possible and praying it wasn't too late for us to have a second chance. That he'd forgive me for the perpetual seesaw I'd been on lately.

Reaching a stoplight, I pulled my cell out of my purse and fired off a quick text.

ME:

> Is two apology texts in so many weeks bad form? Is it too late for us? Please tell me it isn't.

Placing my phone on the center console, I held my breath, hoping for a response. Just as the light turned green, three little dots appeared below my sent message, sparking a glimmer of hope inside me.

I stepped on the gas, checking my cell every few seconds, waiting for his reply. The wail of approaching sirens grew closer, and I glanced in my rearview mirror. When I didn't see any flashing lights, I continued through the intersection, stealing a final look at my cell.

But before I could merge onto the freeway, a black SUV came speeding out of nowhere, slamming into the passenger side door, my car spinning out of control.

Tires squealed. Glass shattered. Metal crunched.

Then everything went dark.

CHAPTER THIRTY-THREE

Gideon

"What did I miss?" I asked as I entered the suite after sitting through a gourmet five-course meal with the who's who of politics delivering grandiose speeches about their supposed accomplishments.

In reality, all they were good at was spending money that wasn't theirs.

Despite my itching desire to leave, I stayed for dinner, not wanting to raise anyone's suspicions. After all, I'd paid a half-million dollars for the privilege of being in that room.

That didn't stop James from leaving immediately following our conversation, though.

While I would have loved for him to stick around for

the real fireworks, I knew it was a strong possibility he'd slip out once I confronted him.

"He's panicking," Henry replied with a grin. "Especially now that the audio recording is making headlines."

That was another reason I wanted to stay at the fundraiser — to see everyone's reactions as the headlines starting coming in.

As I expected, the president ended up canceling his appearance in order to do damage control.

After all, James Turner was a high-ranking member of his party. This sort of thing could have a disastrous impact on everyone connected to him, especially in an election year.

"But it looks like bad publicity is about to be the least of his worries." Henry nodded at a monitor placed on the mahogany desk, its screen displaying footage from a security feed of James' Brentwood home that Henry had hacked into.

A dark sedan crept along the driveway and parked in front of the lavish house, unmarked but clearly law enforcement, a fact I confirmed when a pair of men stepped out, their ill-fitting suits and no-nonsense posture screaming cop.

It didn't escape James' notice, either.

He paused for a few seconds, his eyes fixated on a monitor on his desk containing what I assumed to be the security feed.

When the two men approached the front door, he rushed to a safe on the opposite wall and hurriedly opened it, shoving wads of cash into a duffel bag.

"This is such a cliché," I said with a chuckle, shaking my head. "How far does he think he'll get with the cops knocking on his door? You don't think he's stupid enough to make a run for it with the police right there. Do you?"

"At this point, nothing would surprise me," Henry replied.

Sure enough, just as one of the cops knocked, James darted through the house and into the attached garage, climbing into a dark SUV.

Seconds later, the garage door opened and James peeled out, driving over flowerbeds and his perfectly manicured lawn in order to make a hasty escape.

My stomach twisted in discomfort as I watched the cops rush back to their car and speed after James.

This was not how I envisioned things playing out.

I'd wanted him to endure a public scandal.

Wanted him to feel helpless as his world fell apart around him.

Wanted every news station to show footage of him being led away in handcuffs for the world to see.

I'd considered every angle and had decided on this plan of action.

After all, for a man like James, character assassination and prison *were* worse than death.

I hadn't expected him to flee.

What made matters worse was that I'd seen him consume enough scotch to make him even more reckless than he already was.

"Didn't OJ teach these assholes anything?" Henry mused, hitting a few buttons on his keyboard.

The speakers crackled to life with the sound of police chatter, broadcasting their pursuit of James.

I grabbed the remote and navigated to a local station. Within moments, they interrupted their regularly scheduled program with a breaking news report about a high-speed chase.

Only in LA did they turn a police pursuit into a spectacle worthy of prime-time television.

Then again, it wasn't every day a U.S. Senator ran from the cops after a recording implicating him in serious criminal activity was released.

I held my breath as James weaved in and out of traffic for several miles, his massive SUV slicing through the sea of cars with reckless abandon.

The police pursued him to the best of their ability, but they also had to keep public safety in mind, driving cautiously compared to James' wild maneuvers.

A voice over the radio feed mentioned trying to shut down the 405 at the Sepulveda Pass and deploying spike strips at strategic points, but it would take a little longer to put these measures into action. In the meantime, one of the pursuing cars would try to get close enough to shoot out a tire.

My phone buzzed in my pocket, and I retrieved it, expecting it to be a news alert about the police chase.

To my surprise, it was a text from Imogene.

After our last conversation, I didn't think I'd hear from her again.

I clicked on the message, worried she was in trouble, especially now that I hadn't been keeping a constant eye on her, leaving that responsibility to Henry's team.

Thankfully, it had nothing to do with her safety. Instead, it had everything to do with us.

IMOGENE:

Is two apology texts in so many weeks bad form? Is it too late for us? Please tell me it isn't.

I stared at her words, unsure how to feel about them.

On one hand, I didn't want to cause her any more pain than I already had.

On the other, I couldn't deny it felt like something was missing this week. But did that change anything? I wasn't sure if it could.

Not anymore.

Still, Imogene deserved to know how I felt about her. How I'd *always* feel about her, no matter the path I chose.

ME:

My love for you is and always will be unconditional.

I hit send, then returned my attention to the TV as James' vehicle approached Wilshire Boulevard at a high rate of speed without a single care for the fact that he had a red light.

"Fuck," I exhaled when I noticed another dark SUV sitting at the light that just turned green.

I could only pray the driver heard the helicopter or sirens and stayed put.

But they didn't.

The scene played out in slow motion as James' SUV sped ahead at the same time as the other car moved forward.

"Faster, faster," I hissed, unsure which car I was talking to.

I couldn't stomach the idea of an innocent person getting hurt.

It was only supposed to be James.

No one else.

But as my eyes remained glued to the television, a sinking feeling formed in my gut that I wouldn't get my wish, which was confirmed when James' car slammed into the passenger side of the SUV, the speed at which he hit it causing it to spin out of control until coming to a stop several yards away.

Heaviness weighed on my chest as the news continued to broadcast a live feed of the aftermath, but I barely heard a word they said, my guilt drowning out everything else.

It wasn't supposed to happen like this.

James was supposed to feel helpless as he lost everything. A cop was supposed to go to his house and arrest him.

The media was supposed to repeatedly show footage of him being led into the police station in handcuffs.

He wasn't supposed to make a run for it.

And he certainly wasn't supposed to go on a high-speed chase through Santa Monica in his intoxicated state before slamming into another car, turning it into nothing but a pile of metal and broken glass.

I tried to convince myself I wasn't to blame. That James made the choice to run from the police.

Still, I couldn't ignore the nagging voice telling me I was the one who set these wheels in motion. That my obsession with revenge now caused an innocent person to get hurt.

Or worse.

It was one thing to take the lives of the men who plotted my demise.

But this?

I wasn't sure if I'd ever forgive myself for this.

"Can you... Can you find out who owns that car?" I asked Henry, pushing down the bile rising in my throat.

"It might take a bit. I don't have anything to go on. Let me see if I can get a closeup of the plate."

"Thanks." I looked back at the screen, police and fire-fighters swarming the scene to deliver aid.

I feared it would be too late.

"Oh god..." Henry quivered, the color draining from his face as he shifted his gaze toward me.

"What is it?"

He didn't say anything, just stared at me with parted lips, his normally easy-going demeanor nowhere to be found.

"Whose car is it, Henry?" I demanded, panic over-taking me the longer I looked at the pity in his eyes.

The room grew thick with tension, the sound of my racing heart echoing in my ears.

In my life, there had been several moments that stood out. That I'd always remember.

Seeing Liam point a gun at me.

Killing a man for the first time.

Finally escaping the prison I'd been in for years.

But this moment would always shine brighter than all the rest.

Because this was the moment I realized the true cost of my need for revenge.

Henry swallowed hard, his voice barely audible as he uttered the one name I didn't want to hear.

"Imogene Prescott."

Thank you for reading *Tempting Devil*! I hope you enjoyed this installment of Gideon and Imogene's story.

Will Gideon give up his plans now that he finally realizes the true price of his revenge? Find out today in the epic conclusion, *Final Vendetta*.

The man I used to be can't save her.
And the monster I've become might destroy us both.

https://geni.us/Vendetta-back

Thanks again for taking the time to read this book. If you enjoyed it, please let your friends know by leaving a review so more people can fall in love with Gideon and Imogene.

FINAL VENDETTA

For five years, vengeance fueled me, keeping me alive through the darkness.

Every move I made was calculated. Every step brought me closer to the justice stolen from me.

But I didn't see the cost. Not until it was too late.

My actions have put Imogene's life in danger.

The man I used to be can't save her.

And the monster I've become might destroy us both.

Now, the line between right and wrong is blurred beyond recognition, and the clock is ticking. One wrong move will cost me everything... Imogene, my redemption, and the future I never thought I could have.

They say love demands sacrifice. But how much more am I willing to lose?

Scan below or type the address into your web browser.

https://geni.us/Vendetta-back

ACKNOWELDGMENTS

I have a confession to make. The second book in a trilogy is always the hardest book for me to write. While the first book certainly has its challenges, because it often takes me a bit to settle on a premise, it's the second book that offers the most challenge, at least for me. The first book sets everything up. The last book wraps everything up. But the second book... That's the meat of the story and where the conflict can really shine. Which is why I really wanted to make you all see just how much Imogene struggled with learning the truth and Gideon struggled with telling her.

Secretly, I love books like this. When the reader knows something the character doesn't and is just waiting for that bomb to drop. Originally, I had a different plan for how Imogene would confirm her suspicions about who Gideon was, but as I should be used to by now, my characters had their own opinion, and I just went with it. And I'm thrilled how it turned out. I hope you are too!

Before I go, I wanted to thank a few people for all their help.

First and foremost, a huge thanks to my husband, Stan, and my daughter, Harper Leigh. I couldn't do this without their support.

To my wonderful PA, Melissa Crump — many thanks for everything you do for me.

To my fantastic beta readers — Lin, Melissa, Sylvia, Stacy, and Vicky — thanks for always reading and offering feedback.

To my admin team — Melissa and Vicky. Thanks for keeping my reader group and page running. Love you ladies!

To my review team — Thank you for always not only reading my books but also taking the time to write reviews. With the amount of books out there today, I'm grateful you're on my team.

To my reader group — Thanks for being my super-fans and giving me a place to go when I need a break from writing.

And last but not least, a big thank you to YOU — my amazing readers. I'm so grateful for your support. Can't wait to share the final chapter of Imogene and Gideon's story with you. Buckle up! It's going to be a bumpy ride.

Love & Peace,
   ~ T.K.

ABOUT THE AUTHOR

T.K. Leigh is a *USA Today* Bestselling author of romance ranging from fun and flirty to sexy and suspenseful.

Originally from New England, she now resides just outside of Raleigh with her husband, beautiful daughter, rescued special needs dog, and three cats. When she's not writing, she can be found training for her next marathon or chasing her daughter around the house.

facebook.com/tkleighauthor

instagram.com/tkleigh

tiktok.com/@tkleigh

bookbub.com/authors/t-k-leigh

pinterest.com/tkleighauthor

www.ingramcontent.com/pod-product-compliance
Lightning Source LLC
Chambersburg PA
CBHW011128190726
48289CB00012B/2952